Sunlit Riffles and Shadowed Runs

Terrace Books, a trade imprint of the University of Wisconsin Press, takes its name from the Memorial Union Terrace, located at the University of Wisconsin–Madison. Since its inception in 1907, the Wisconsin Union has provided a venue for students, faculty, staff, and alumni to debate art, music, politics, and the issues of the day. It is a place where theater, music, drama, literature, dance, outdoor activities, and major speakers are made available to the campus and the community. To learn more about the Union, visit www.union.wisc.edu.

Sunlit Riffles and Shadowed Runs

Stories of Fly Fishing in America

Kent Cowgill

Terrace Books
A trade imprint of the University of Wisconsin Press

Terrace Books
A trade imprint of the University of Wisconsin Press
1930 Monroe Street, 3rd Floor
Madison, Wisconsin 53711-2059
uwpress.wisc.edu

3 Henrietta Street
London WCE 8LU, England
eurospanbookstore.com

Printed in the United States of America

Library of Congress Cataloging-in-Publication Data
Cowgill, Kent.
Sunlit riffles and shadowed runs : stories of fly fishing in America / Kent Cowgill.
      p.   cm.
ISBN 978-0-299-28910-2 (cloth: alk. paper)
ISBN 978-0-299-28913-3 (e-book)
1. Fly fishing—United States—Fiction. I. Title.
PS3553.O9115S86 2012
813'.54—dc23
2012012024

This is a work of fiction. Any references to historical events, to real people living or dead, to real
locales are intended only to give the fiction a setting in historical reality. Other names, characters,
places, and incidents are either the product of the author's imagination or are used fictitiously, and
their resemblance, if any, to real-life counterparts is entirely coincidental.

A few of these stories were first published in *Fly Rod & Reel* magazine: "Coachmen" (July/October
1990, published as "Coachman"), "Day of Mourning" (July/October 1994), "Indian Summer"
(July/October 1995), "Spanish Fly" (July/October 1997), and "Two Men in a Museum" (Autumn
2010, Traver Award winner). "Season's End" was first published in *Trout* magazine (Autumn
1990).

Dedicated to

Scott, my brother,

whose love, faith, kindness, and boundless courage

showed all of us how a life should be lived.

Now as he looked down the river, the insects must be settling on the surface, for the trout were feeding steadily all down the stream. As far down the long stretch as he could see, the trout were rising, making circles all down the surface of the water, as though it were starting to rain.

Ernest Hemingway, "Big Two-Hearted River"

Contents

Acknowledgments

Any fly fisher who is honest, if that's not an oxymoron, is indebted to far too many people to count. The same is true, perhaps even truer, of one who writes. With sincere apologies to the many big-hearted individuals whom space constraints have not let me mention here, I want to thank the following for their friendship, tip sharing, and otherwise invaluable contributions to my writing and angling life:

My wife, Jane, whose love, grace, artistic insight, and indulgence of my more than occasional foibles and fixations I can never sufficiently repay.

Mike Meeker, Joe Kolupke, Orval Lund, Scott Bestul, and Jane Cowgill for their generous critical feedback on several of the stories in this collection, and all five of them, together with Bruce Johnson, James Nichols, John Cowgill, Nelson and Leif Rasmuson, Dr. Donna Crosley, Chuck Shepard, Jerry Seim, Bruce Fuller, Dave Mahlke, Paul Ballweg, Jerry Heymans, John Short, Dr. Hans Zinnecker, Jim Johnson, the crew members of *Very like a Whale*, and the late Bob Briggs and Hub Bambenek for all you've done to enrich my years on rivers and streams. The magic of fly fishing has flowed into my soul through many of your capable hands.

Jim Butler, Joe Healy, and the current and former staff at *Fly Rod & Reel* magazine for having published several of the collection's stories in its annual Traver Award fiction contest. Also, *Trout* magazine and

Acknowledgments

Trout Unlimited for publishing in 1990 one of my earliest fly fishing stories, "Season's End."

Dennis Johnson, for his artistic talents.

Paul A. Olson, Ed Hahn, and Kent Eakins, whose generosity and goodwill are expressions of what I value most about Nebraska, my home state.

My sons, Eric and Andy, for the countless ways they have encouraged and supported me. Their interest in my tales, oral and written, has been a creative stimulus since their childhood days in Camp Winnebago, Cluny Cottage, and the old camping van Aunt Pettitoes.

My brothers, Doug and Scott, for a shared lifetime of joyous experiences on streams, fields, courts, and other venues dating back to our own cramped childhood bedrooms in the tiny village whose apt name, Silver Creek, I could only later come to appreciate.

My mother, Barbara—ageless, heartwarming matriarch.

John Gierach, for his generous help and advice.

Bob White, for the beautiful painting that graces this book's cover.

And finally, the terrific professional staff at the University of Wisconsin Press, especially Raphael Kadushin, Matthew Cosby, Adam Mehring, Andrea Christofferson, Anne McKenna, Carla Marolt, Francine Grogan, and Diana Cook, for your many attentive contributions. Working with all of you has been one of the most rewarding experiences of my life.

Sunlit Riffles and Shadowed Runs

Day of Mourning

The coffin had been laid to rest with such dispatch its burnished image lingered on in the mind's eye, the russet wood glazed with sunlight, the varnish on its bevels gleaming with a lustrous sheen.

The widow approached us in the reception hall a few minutes later, long limbed and shapely beneath her black dress.

"So it's you three," she said coolly. "The companions of his riotous youth." Her eyes glistened behind the tracery of her veil.

"Our condolences, ma'am," Barry said.

She turned away, toward the table, where other women were filling cups from a punch bowl. Her fingers tightened beneath her soft linen gloves.

"He was a fine man," Hap offered, his voice the texture of sawdust.

"None better," Barry added.

"He was an asshole," the widow said.

Hap nodded awkwardly. "That too," he mumbled, swallowing. "A man of parts."

Muffled clothing whispered behind us. The ladle clinked dully against the rim of the crystal bowl.

"You'll forgive me if I don't stay to reminisce," the widow said, turning. "I don't mean to be rude. But it's unlikely I'd be very responsive to the experiences you shared with him."

"We understand," I murmured.

She stepped away, then turned back to face us. "I nearly forgot," she added. "There's something he mentioned in those last few minutes when he was drifting in and out of consciousness. I'm embarrassed to repeat it, frankly. But I suppose no matter how trivial, his last wishes deserve to be passed along."

We waited for her to go on.

"He wanted you to have his fishing pole."

I glanced at my companions, their backs rigid as a pair of steel posts. Hap's left eyelid began to twitch.

"Which one?" he managed to mumble. The two syllables sounded as if they'd been force fed through his larynx. "Is it the—?" He caught himself and stopped. "If I remember," he croaked, "Charlie had eight or ten."

"I'm not certain. Can it possibly make any difference? It wasn't until just before his last breath that he mentioned the thing at all. He started rambling on about how I could keep everything else, but his pole should go to 'HapSkiporBarry.'"

She paused, eyeing us through the veil as if we were the Three Stooges. Finally she went on.

"He didn't say anything about there being several of them, or even make it clear what your names were. You might have been some breakfast cereal, for all I knew."

She drifted away toward the punch bowl, returned a few moments later with her cup half filled.

"It doesn't surprise me to learn that he had so many of those things. That was Charlie. Whatever he did, he did to excess. I shudder to think what I'm going to discover when I go down to his den and start sorting for the garage sale. He had enou—"

She stopped short, her eyes dropping to the drops of punch my trembling hands had spilled on the carpet. "You needn't worry," she added accusingly. "I'll let you have the newest one."

Hap took a strangled sip from his own cup. My eyes were fixed on the quivering saucer in his hand.

"We couldn't do that, ma'am," he croaked. "Wouldn't be right. It's been years since any of us fished with him. You sell his newest ones at the sale. I suspect it was one of the older rods he had in mind."

"Are you sure he didn't describe it?" Barry prompted her, tugging at his collar. "Tell you where you could find it down in that den?" I'd never seen Barry in a tie before. His face was the color of a ripe plum.

4

"I don't believe so, no."

"Didn't say anything about 'the old buggy whip'?"

"No."

"His 'sweet little split-cane flagellator'?"

She grimaced—looked around the room as if searching for a mourner from the vice squad.

"*The Payne?*" I blurted. "Did he ever say anything about *the Payne?*"

"Yes!" she said. "That's it! I remember because I was thinking how odd it was that he didn't seem to be experiencing any. He just lay there, babbling on, but serene. Then he said it, just before he died. 'Give them the pain.'"

"Jesus," Hap croaked.

We had buttoned our coats, were heading for the door, when the widow intercepted us in the hall.

"You all ran off before I had a chance to finish," she said icily. "As if that were the last tray of sandwiches anyone was going to set out." She paused, then went on. "It was hard to make out his last words, but I did grasp a few of them, enough to know there were a couple of conditions. One was that if all three of you came to his funeral, he wanted the pole to go to the first one who could use the thing to catch a twelve-pound trout."

"*What!*" Barry bellowed. Pie crumbs sprinkled his beard as his crazed eyes swept the hushed room's stunned, upturned faces. "I mean," he stumbled on in a hoarse whisper, "are you sure he said a twelve-*pound* trout?"

"Yes . . . no . . . maybe it was twelve *inches*, now that I think about it. Would that seem more likely? I'll admit, I wasn't paying a lot of attention at that point. Seriously, let's be honest, anybody who knew Charlie would know his dying words weren't destined for Bartlett's list of memorable quotations. But to leave the world thinking about some fishing pole, and harassing the nurse for a shot of Jim Beam?"

Barry nodded understandingly. "That was ole Chuck, for damned sure," he mumbled. "Sorry, ma'am," he added reddening. "Alls I meant was he had to be suffering. Prob'ly needed that shot just to dull the pain."

5

"It was twelve *inches*," Hap pronounced definitively. "No doubt about it. Even in some deathbed delusion, Charlie couldn't have got within double-haul distance of a twelve-pound trout."

Barry and I nodded in silent affirmation. I turned back to the widow. "What's the other condition?" I ventured, afraid to ask.

She took a slow sip from her punch cup. "You have to catch the fish in 'the Whitewater.' I take it that's a river not far from here."

I stared blankly at my two fellow pallbearers, whose expressions were appropriately funereal. "More a creek than a river," Barry finally responded, clearly as relieved as I was. "I fished it with him ten or twelve years ago. It's a pain in the rear, but I guess we'll have to agree on a date when we can all fly back this summer and get 'er done."

Hap shook his head cheerlessly, contemplating the prospect. His scarf drooped like black crepe beneath his chin.

The widow stared at us for a moment, smiling faintly. "You seem to have misunderstood," she said. "You don't need to wait until the summer. In fact, you *can't* wait that long, not if you actually do want this old pole of his. That's the one thing I understood perfectly. He clutched my arm as he said it. *The day after my funeral!* You have to catch the fish tomorrow."

"Tomorrow!"

The word fell from our lips like a block of ice. Turning, the three of us peered as one out the window. Four feet of snow blanketed the Minnesota landscape. A thin skein of white smoke hung above a chimney across the ice-glazed street as if struggling to free itself from the bricks.

"Jesus," Hap said again.

No one said anything as the widow nodded good-bye—left us staring numbly through the frosted glass as she rejoined the other women. Barry tugged his gloves on abstractedly. Hap fumbled with the collar button on his coat.

"Tomorrow."

"When I stepped off the plane last night, it was eighteen degrees below zero," Barry murmured. "It felt like somebody was pounding a railroad spike through my brain."

At ten the next morning, after we had thawed the rental car's battery, pillaged Charlie's den for warmer clothes, and piled the car to the roof with our plunder from the local Goodwill and Salvation Army, the three of us sat in a local café, steeling ourselves for the hours ahead. Hap asked the waitress to bring a pot of coffee to a full boil, then pour all of it straight into his thermos. Barry told her to make his a double, and add a large shot of scotch. I stared down at the last leathery slice of bread on my plate.

"I'd like a couple of pieces of waxed paper," I said to her. "No hurry. Just bring them when you give one of these guys the check."

"Waxed paper?" Barry said dubiously.

"I'm taking this french toast," I said. "At least that's what they called it on the menu. I may not eat it, but it's another inch of insulation over my heart."

Hap nodded. "Nick Adams," he said. "Big Two-Hearted River . . . I fished it once. Up in the UP."

"That was a sandwich," I corrected him. "And he was fishing in July."

The road to the stream was memorable for a couple of reasons: It was covered with so much packed snow that trying to steer the car was pointless, and steering would have been irrelevant anyway since both ditches were drifted so high the vehicle rolled between them the way a kid's bowling ball rolls down a lane with rails. Hap, nominally the driver, finally just put it in cruise control at ten mph and rolled on.

It was noon when Barry finally directed him to a sliding stop, our mittened hands fumbling at the door handles as if they were the hatch latches of a space capsule. In truth, the whole experience seemed lunar. I had added so many layers of clothing I moved with the stiff-legged stagger of a fat astronaut. Hap, who had dug to the bottom of a Goodwill barrel, wore a black woolen mask that made him look like a porcine Darth Vader. Barry was struggling into a pair of chest waders he'd bought at a local sporting goods store, the biggest they had, size sixteen. They barely fit over the mélange of unmixed socks he'd pulled out of the same barrel, though his normal shoe size is ten.

The sunlight off the snow was so incandescent it burned the eyes—disoriented all sense of perception. Lowering my cap brim, I peered back through the open door, down at the Spanish mahogany rod case that lay on the front seat between the pair of thermoses. The patina on its dovetailed cuts was as bright as the gleam off their steel lids.

I turned back to the others.

"This fish," I said. "Did she actually *specify* what rod we have to catch it on?"

Barry looked up morosely. His breath had already formed icicles on his beard. "Where the hell were you?" he said. "The Payne goes to whoever uses it to take a twelve-pou—. *Damn*," he stopped. "I still haven't shaken it. A twelve-*inch* trout."

He peered down at the coveted rod case. Breath continued to pour like puffs of steam from his mouth.

I looked away.

"It's like taking a Stradivarius into a karaoke bar," I murmured. "Even stringing it in this weather would qualify as indecent exposure in most states."

No one responded. A gust of wind sledge-hammered my forehead as the three of us stood numb on the frozen road.

"Wait a minute!" Hap said suddenly. At least I assumed it was Hap. The voice seemed to come from somewhere behind that black mask down the hooded tunnel of his parka. "I'm trying to remember exactly what she said. Wasn't it 'the first one of you who could use *the thing* to catch a trout'?"

He nodded toward the car seat, bent down, and picked up the rod case as he went on. "I don't know about you boys, but what I'm holding here sure as hell couldn't be described as *the thing*."

"I'm hearin' you," Barry grunted. "*The thing* is what I saw you slip in the trunk back at her house—that whippy old eight-weight he told us was great for pike and bass."

If a man can look sheepish in a mask and wolfskin mittens, Hap did. But he recovered quickly. It was so cold a virgin nudist could have come up with the requisite sangfroid. "I was just preserving it for posterity," he mumbled. "If you noticed, that stack of kindling by her fireplace was getting damned low."

"That's about all you preserved, a little kindling," Barry shot back. "But it's gonna be tough to light it. Go take a look. Take it out of its sleeve." Hap stared at him, then shuffled back to the rear of the car. We watched as he fumbled with the keys, chipped off a layer of ice and pried the trunk open, then slammed it a half-dozen times before the frozen catch finally caught. The sound echoed across the gelid landscape like rifle fire.

He shuffled back to us holding a two-piece, fiberglass nine-footer. The wraps were frayed. A guide was missing. The grip looked as if it had been gnawed by a mouse.

"No question," I said. "That's *the thing*. That's the rod she meant."

Hap reached for the thermoses, dropped them in a tote bag, and slung it glumly over his shoulder. "You got his fly box?" he croaked at Barry. "Somewhere under all those layers, Skip's wearing his vest."

"It's between the flannel pajamas and the Vikings sweatsuit," I said. "But I don't think it has an ice auger. Don't ask me to check."

I intended it as a grim joke. It turned out to be grim enough—the Reaper might have loved it—but a joke it wasn't. When we'd waddled the dozen yards to the bridge—stared down at the stream we'd been sentenced to fish—what stretched below us was a snow-shrouded ribbon of glare ice.

For at least a minute no one spoke.

Eventually Hap offered an anesthetized reflection. "The White-water," he croaked through his mask. "Not hard to see how the damned thing got its name."

Barry pried a frozen rock from the road and flipped it dejectedly down toward what even a lunatic leap of faith couldn't construe as a habitat for *Salmo trutta*. The rock bounced and skidded crazily away into the snow.

"Toughest day to read the water I've ever seen," he said.

But we hit the river. It was the first time in my three decades of trout fishing the expression was literal. Rapping our way upstream with a stick—or at least moving in the direction Barry thought he recalled was upstream—we shuffled over the ice toward a dark, ragged-edged seam of water that glinted surreally on the horizon. Despite the blinding sun, the snow cracked like breaking bones under our boots.

In the car, we had matched coins to determine the casting order, agreeing to continue in sequence until one of us had landed the jackpot fish. Hap had won the honors. As we approached the tiny swatch of open water, Barry asked him what fly he was going to tie on.

Wheezing, the angler stopped a few feet short of what only a winter-shocked Bedouin could have called a pool. His breath hung in crystallized shards from the ski mask. The seam stretched for a hundred narrow yards ahead of him like a crevasse on a glacial field.

I never learned what pattern he'd intended to start with. By the time he'd managed to string the rod, shed his mittens, and loop a crude granny knot around a 2X tippet, the decision had been rendered as moot as any movement in his fingers. The fly that finally dangled below the rod tip was the box's largest—a battered Woolly Bugger with an oversized eye. The hands that had somehow affixed it to the stiffened leader shivered their way back into the mittens like a pair of hairless white rats.

Ten minutes and as many stunned gulps of coffee later, he had recovered enough to move on. Barry and I huddled behind him as he crept into position to make the first cast, his padded frame hunched beneath the fur-fringed parka. The rod in his mittened hand looked as incongruous as a conductor's baton in the paw of a bear.

Like everything attached to my body, time froze over the next hour, which the three of us spent alternating casts in a Sherpa-like pilgrimage toward the head of the ice-wreathed pool. Never has a fly more accurately been described as "dead drifted," despite an involuntary countermove every few seconds that caused the fisherman's goose-fleshed anatomy to quiver in a spastic twitch. No more than two minutes had passed before the rod's weight could have been measured on a truck scale. We were barely into our third cycle, had made fewer than ten casts, before the line was sheathed in so much ice it rattled like a rusty chain through the rod guides. If Minnesota trout were drawn to the clacking of a corn sheller, we were about to have a hell of an afternoon.

Handing Hap the ponderous rig for his next cast, I felt obliged to warn him. "Now you're fishing with a lead core," I muttered. "Just sayin'. You might not want to get too fancy with that thing."

The words congealed in the polar air. He raised the rod, made a single false cast, and staggered a half-step forward as he slipped on a patch of ice. The ice-weighted line came within an inch of cold-cocking him as it hissed like a length of steel cable past his right ear. The sound when it slapped the water reverberated all the way back to the bridge.

"I think you might've put 'em down," Barry said drolly. "If any of 'em are dumb enough to be out in this weather. Anyways, it don't count if the fly kills one by hittin' it on the head."

It was my turn when we ran out of open water, about the time the bearings began to freeze in the reel. Nothing but arctic tundra stretched ahead of us as far as my bleared eyes could see.

I gazed longingly back toward the road, the car, only its radio antenna visible above a snowbank. I tried to convince myself that the priceless rod inside that gleaming box on the front seat was worth yielding to the demented impulse assailing my brain.

My padded companions were slouching back toward the vehicle like a pair of forlorn Michelin men when they realized I wasn't following. By the time they'd shuffled to a stop, stood staring back at me, my mittens were off and my pocketknife lay clutched in a shivering hand.

"You're a better man than I am," Hap wheezed, his outsized boots creaking as he retraced his steps. "Just be sure before you cut that damned fly off you've got something else you're going to be able to knot on."

I paused, reflecting, then shed my liner gloves. In the time it took me to free the knife blade my exposed flesh began to mummify. Clasping the Woolly Bugger between two unfeeling digits, I began paring off its parts from barb to eye.

"What the hell?" Barry said.

I shaved it down to the bare shank. Then I pawed through my layers of clothing until I found what felt like Charlie's vest, though it was hard to tell with fingers the color and temperature of a vanilla Popsicle.

11

Somehow they came out holding the tube of split shot I was groping for.

"*What the hell?*" Hap said.

Nursing the few seconds of blood flow I had remaining, I tooth-clamped a pair of the shot onto the leader while a dozen more fell into the snow. Moaning, I plunged my petrified palms back into my mittens and clamped them for a time under my armpits. No matter how long the rest of it took, the mittens weren't coming off again. Frostbite was a given, but I was damned if I was going to go as far as gangrene. A man with amputated arms would have a hell of a hard time holding a fly rod, even one as sweet as a Payne.

By the time I'd extracted the slice of french toast from my shirt, toe-nudged it onto the ice, and somehow managed to slice off a small chunk to dress the pared hook shank, the faint pulsings I occasionally felt behind my glassy eyeballs were the only signs of life rising from the outlying provinces I'd once known as my hands.

"You're usin' *that?*" Barry bellowed. "You're gonna fish *bait?*"

"Hell, no!" I mumbled. "Bait's a night crawler. Dough balls. One of those big salmon egg clusters I know you always keep hidden in an inside pocket of your vest. This is a cross between a Breadcrust Nymph and a Parmachene Belle no-hackle. I call it the French Kiss."

"But it's not . . . it's not *decent*," Hap protested.

I swung the rig out over the water and let the split shot drag the syrup-soaked hunk back under the shelf of ice. The current sucked it downstream under our feet.

"This is the Big One," I said to them. "When the foundation's shaking and your goddamned bed's covered with roof plaster, you don't hang around looking for your slippers and a robe."

Ten yards below me the hook hung up on the gravel bottom. Following, I tugged it free and let the glutinous toast drift on.

"That's it," Hap said, grabbing my elbow. "Your turn is over. Now I get a crack with that thing."

I pulled away, punctuating the point with an upstream mend. "*Cretin!*" I shouted. "I don't know where you've been doing your worm-dunking, but where I angle, the cast isn't over until the fly lifts off the stream."

Twenty yards farther on, the line halted again, seemed faintly to throb. The sheath of ice above the leader strained like an anchor rope in the current. Then, almost imperceptibly, I felt the rod dip in my hand. I jerked back instinctively, my brain frozen, my right arm shooting toward the sky like a beleaguered umpire's signaling a game-ending out. A brown trout flew out of the water over my head and lay gasping behind us on the snow.

"*Yes!*" I yawped toward the distant blufftops. "That's *it!* That's *the one!*"

Barry gaped at me, his ice-lidded eyes milky with envy. Then he gaped down at the fish. I saw his hand plunge deep in the pocket of his parka. It emerged half a minute later with a tape measure clutched in his gloved fist. Hap's eyes were rolling maniacally behind his ski mask. Shuddering, both of them dropped to their knees.

They pulled the tape so tight it creaked as they stretched it over the fish, its body already rigid. Its eyes could have been mistaken for white marbles. The gape of its open mouth looked like Munch's *The Scream.* The tape's diamond oscillated over the trout's nose. "*Eleven and three-quarter inches!*" Hap whooped. "*Close, but no cigar!*"

"Could be eleven and seven-eighths," Barry allowed. "Give or take. Too damned bad, but it ain't quite enough."

I turned away toward the road, then back to the fish—saw its gaping jaws open even wider in Munchian stupefaction. Sighing, I pulled my camera out of my knapsack. My own eyelashes had ringed with a frozen rosary of beaded tears.

"It's twelve," I said. "At least it was before you measured it. Here. Get its picture before you slide it back into the water, to show the widow. . . . We can share the rod," I added in resignation, "the same way we've used this one. Each of us keeps it for a year. *But I go first!*"

I didn't say anything on the way back to the car. Barry mumbled something about the fish possibly being fourteen or fifteen inches long when it came out of the water—said we were each probably half a foot shorter ourselves, if you factored in how much things shrank in subzero weather. Hap stumbled on ahead of us, stiff legged, his arms splayed like the flightless wings of a penguin. Once or twice I thought I heard him croak, "The Payne, the Payne!"

13

Two Men in a Museum

"None of his paintings work for me," the woman said, her finger pointing at a winding band of silver running diagonally across a background that looked to her husband like a thick stand of pine. "It's basically a trick, trying to obscure how labored and derivative the naturalism is by imposing this abstract pewter swatch across the canvas. Turner did it two hundred years ago, and about that many times more creatively."

The retired lawyer sat on a bench in the middle of the small room, watching them. The woman was thin, attractive, though she'd have been far more so with longer hair and clothes that were less dowdy. He pegged her as an academic. Of her male companion, probably her husband, he wasn't so sure.

"I don't know," the man answered, smiling nonchalantly. "I kind of like it. Maybe because that slash of silver reminds me of a good trout stream."

The couple appeared to be in their midforties, perhaps fifty, and were clearly not from the city. The lawyer continued to study them, eavesdropping. He had retired two years earlier at seventy, his wife had died suddenly a few months later, and he'd spent most of his days since then restless and bored, idly searching for ways other than drinking to kill time. People watching absorbed him far more than the squirrels and birds of Central Park, and art museums were among his preferred sites.

"You're hopeless," the woman said, shaking her head at her blond-bearded, curly-haired companion. A thin smile took the edge off the barb. "I've seen enough," she added. "Let's go up to the third floor. I want to see the Berninis and the Ghirlandaios."

"You go on ahead," the man murmured. "I'll find you. I think I'll hang out down here a few minutes more."

He laid his hand on her shoulder with a familiarity that told the observing lawyer he was unmistakably her husband. His gaze remained on the couple as the woman left the room, his eyes dropping to the open book resting on his lap only when the husband turned and stared.

When the lawyer glanced up again a few seconds later the man's eyes were still on him. A faint grin creased his large, ruddy face.

"Mind if I plop down myself for a few minutes?" he asked abruptly. "My wife could do this all day, but I'm good for about an hour. I don't think the legs ever get tireder than they do from gallery fatigue."

"Sit, by all means," the lawyer answered, closing the book and shifting slightly on the bench. He studied the stranger more closely as he shuffled over and eased down beside him. Unruly hair. A solid frame. Scuffed shoes beneath off-the-rack pants and a tan corduroy jacket. In his Savile Row suit and silk tie, the older man felt a flash of superiority, urban pride.

"I take it you're a fisherman," he said, glad nonetheless for the momentary company. He tried to keep any trace of condescension out of his voice.

The stranger stared again at him briefly, surprised, then smiled with sudden recognition.

"You heard what I said to my wife, eh, about that painting," he chuckled, his face coloring. "Sorry. I'm not exactly a barbarian in an art museum, but I'd be lying if I said my tastes went much beyond the Impressionists and the seventeenth-century Dutch."

"I quite agree," the lawyer responded insincerely. In truth, painting didn't interest him at all, though his apartment held half a dozen original works by celebrated contemporary artists his wife had bought with the fruits of his long career on Wall Street.

"Clay Mitchell," the younger man said, extending a meaty hand.

"Fred Corcoran," the lawyer replied, shaking it.

Neither of them said anything more for some time. Finally the lawyer cleared his throat and spoke.

"You and your wife are here from out of town?"

"Yes. From Wisconsin. We're in the same department—history—at a small university in Appleton. There's a conference at Columbia. We ducked out of the early afternoon session. The butt can only take so many papers on what a shortage of goose quills did to the medieval scriptorium."

He laughed again, and the lawyer felt his spirits lift a bit at the midwesterner's odd combination of boondock familiarity and academic verve.

"I *am* a fisherman though, yes," the stranger added, grinning in answer to the conversation-starter the older man had broached. "You too?"

This time it was the lawyer's turn to be surprised. He had never been a fisherman, though as a child he'd fished at his family's vacation home in Maine and had grown skilled enough later in life, mostly out of necessity with well-heeled hosts and clients, to have caught several species on a fly rod at various famed locations in America and abroad. Somehow the sport had never taken. He'd felt little more, landing even the largest fish, than a swell of ego at the impression he knew he'd made on the more experienced anglers at his side.

"Oh, yes, absolutely," he lied.

Pleased at the younger man's fraternal grin, he found himself suddenly floating along on a windy narrative that snatched up every long-forgotten detail he could summon from those guided outings years earlier: a salmon landed on the Miramichi, an afternoon spent stalking large brown trout in New Zealand (had he in fact caught the one they'd netted, or was it Ben Hyman?), the morning he'd hooked and lost a permit (even the odd name of the fish he had to struggle to remember—was it the CEO on the yacht or the black man poling the skiff in Key West who'd mentioned they were even harder to catch than a bonefish?). Half truths and exaggerations, all of them. But when he hobbled to a self-conscious, embarrassed stop, the embarrassment quickly yielded to an even more powerful emotion—acute surprise at how much he had in fact remembered about those far-flung trips, how much more they stirred him now than they had at the time.

"Incredible," the stranger murmured, smiling at him enviously. "What terrific experiences. Most of those are places I always dreamed of fishing, almost from the moment I first read about them thirty-odd years ago, but probably never will."

The lawyer peered into the other man's eyes, misread them completely.

"So you've reached that age too," he said, nodding. "How did Thoreau put it? *The young man goes out fishing, until at last, if he has the seeds of a better life in him, he leaves the fish-pole behind.*"

A long silence fell on the empty room as the historian gazed searchingly at the lawyer, then turned away, toward the painting on the wall.

"That's not what I meant at all," he said softly. "I know the Thoreau passage, and I couldn't disagree with him more, my own experience has been so different. I love fly fishing now as much as I loved it the first time it hooked me, possibly more."

He turned back to the older man as he finished, the passion burning in his florid face. Disconcerted, the lawyer felt his eyes begin to water and his hands tremble in his lap. He had made a sterling career out of his acuity and intelligence—his ability to read people—and the sharp words stunned him, the fact that an apparently competent man of prime earning years could love something as trivial as fishing with the ardor of a child. The fellow was from the hinterlands, that doubtless explained it. An ambitionless hack in some tiny "university" no one who mattered had ever heard of. Regaining his equilibrium, the lawyer cleared his throat and voiced a dismissive response.

"I suppose it happens. Whatever 'turns one on,' as the young say."

It surprised, even slightly offended him, when the other man simply grinned and nodded. The fellow was in truth an even more hapless dolt than he had surmised. In a heartbeat, the lawyer's expectations changed entirely. In place of conversation, there was the prospect of amusement. The latter would momentarily relieve the boredom nearly as well. Only faintly did he recognize the deeper emotion the stranger had stirred in him—the hope, even the need, that he remain seated on the bench. For close to half a century his world had been stability, prosperity, things he knew and could trust. Then within a few months of his retirement came the dizzying whirl of changes that had left his internal compass reeling— his wife's death and the economic meltdown and too many others in a wildly accelerating universe to count. Even three years earlier, he would not have believed it possible that a man of his stature could so quickly be swallowed up, passed by. Banishing the memories with a forced jocularity, he turned back to the stranger and spoke.

"You said something before that intrigues me. Something about 'the moment fly fishing first hooked you,' I believe is how you put it. Be so kind as to tell me, what did you mean?"

The stranger peered back into his eyes with a keenness that cracked wide open his peremptory dismissal of the man's intellect—a gaze the lawyer's own keener instincts recognized instantly as the other man sizing *him* up. Again the room fell silent. After glancing again at the slash of silver bisecting the painting on the wall, the midwesterner replied.

"I grew up on the plains of Kansas," he began quietly, "about as far from trout water as it's possible to get. Did I fish? Sure. Catfish and bullheads mostly—lots of carp none of us back then ever kept. But you're not asking me about that. You're wondering how a man of my age, a so-called academic, can care so much about a sport that didn't genuinely stir you, even during those experiences you described."

He stopped and peered again into the older man's face, the grin on his own still boyish features hardening. The lawyer felt in his gut the folly of his earlier impression. This was a man, if they were seated at a negotiating table, he would not have wanted to face.

"You're right," the lawyer stammered. "I want to know the reason you became a fly fisherman . . . *why* it still means so much to you." Belatedly he realized that the statement, especially its ending, was the truth.

"I loved it once too," he added honestly. "Fished every chance I could get on those family vacations in Maine, back in my childhood. But after college, my life and career here . . ."

His voice trailed off as he glanced up, saw the historian following him intently. "I'm not sure why," he lurched on. "Somewhere in those busy years I came to perceive it much like Thoreau."

It was his own eyes that drifted now to the painting, held there. The abstract belt of silver reminded him too of a river, some forgotten stream in his past. He was still gazing at it when the soft murmur of the stranger's voice reached him, almost hypnotically, once again.

"Back in 1987 I was a first-year graduate student at Michigan, studying medieval history. One of my professors was from Glasgow. At his urging, I spent that summer rattling around Scotland in an old rental camping van. He'd been shrewd enough to see that beneath the hippie hair and false bravado I was a total American hick, greener than a Kansas wheat field. Saw that what I needed far more than two more months cloistered in a library carrel was the experience of simply being abroad. He managed to get me a little grant money for research in Edinburgh, and off I went."

The lawyer continued to stare at the painting. The narrator shifted his bulky body on the bench beside him and resumed.

"I had no idea what to expect, of course. My images of Scotland nearly all came from Robert Burns and *Ivanhoe*. I won't bore you with what I found there, other than to say the experiences turned out to be life changing. And one of the most important was a single morning, in October, when I fished for Atlantic salmon for the first time.

"I said I didn't know much of anything about Scotland, which is true, but I did have a vivid if sketchy awareness of the Atlantic salmon. As a kid, I devoured every issue of *Field & Stream* the day it arrived in our mailbox, and once or twice a year there would be a story or article on this reportedly marvelous fish. I no longer recall any of the pieces specifically, but I do remember some of the references. Most of them were rivers. The *Restigouche*. The one you mentioned, where you caught your salmon, the *Miramichi*. And a rhyming pair in Scotland, the *Tay* and the *Spey*. All of them were magic to me, years before I ever held a fly rod in my hand."

The speaker paused, remembering, as his auditor awkwardly shifted his feet. The lawyer was remembering too—felt his throat go dry with shame at the impulsive lie he'd earlier uttered. The Miramichi salmon had been caught by another fisherman. The truth had flooded back with the midwesterner's trusting openness: the fish darkly visible beneath the shimmering current, too far away for his straining casts to reach it; the forced deference of the Canadian guide, making excuses for him; the shooting arc of the brightly colored fly as the more accomplished fisherman beside him, an investment banker, flicked it elegantly, effortlessly through the air. That the experience had meant nothing to him was another lie, a self-delusion. Just how big a lie began to course through him only now.

"But I had *wanted* to hold one—wanted to own a fly rod—from the moment I read the first of those stories in the magazine."

The swell of humiliation slowly ebbed as the younger man on the bench beside him turned away, went on. "If I hadn't gone to Scotland, in fact, I was going to spend at least part of that summer fishing in the Upper Peninsula, using Hemingway's Nick Adams stories for inspiration . . .

"So anyway, there I was, knocking about alone in a foreign country. I'd tried all the conventional tourist stuff in the first week, after finishing my obligatory research in Edinburgh. Haggis. Single-malt scotch at a distillery. Even bought myself one of those jaunty tweed hats. All of it felt like prologue. What I knew, deep down, that I had come for— the reason I'd agreed so quickly to that Scot professor's urging—was the chance to finally pursue the fish all those articles and stories had convinced me was the noblest, most thrilling fish in the world."

The lawyer nodded and murmured a quiet yes beside him— remembered the image of that great Miramichi salmon hanging over the water, its silver sides flashing in the sun.

"I had no idea how to go about it, of course—even less of the long odds against it ever happening. That's one good thing about being young and naïve, I guess. If I'd been older, known how difficult it was going to be—even known how hard it is simply to get a beat over there on a salmon river—I might never have tried.

"But I knew none of that at the time. I knew only that I was in Scotland, where the famous rivers were, and I was damned sure going to fish one of them with a fly rod or end up dead on my shield."

He laughed self-consciously at the words, the untypical grandilo-quence. Probably only this cherished memory could have swelled such a florid phrase in him. The older man beside him, recalling his own days flaming with youth and ambition on Wall Street, grunted with recognition and waited for the historian to go on.

"And so I set off, searching. The Tay, the Dee, the Spey. They beckoned like the rivers of paradise, but I had neither the tackle nor the streamside beat necessary to fish them. Nor was there any realistic prospect, I soon discovered, of acquiring one. Every inquiry hit the same wall: Private Water. Angling Rights Owned by Lord So-and-so or Such-and-such Club. Poachers Will Be Prosecuted to the Fullest Reach of the Law.

"It seemed futile. I was beaten before setting foot on a beat, a fact as bitter as it was unavoidable. The truth was straight out of a novel I'd recently read called *The Camerons: The lairds own the salmon streams. The lairds own the fish in the sea.*

"I'd wandered through the Highlands for several days, over several hundred miles, when I reached a little town on the far northwest coast named Gairloch. A small hotel appeared on a hill as I rounded a bend on the highway. Discouraged and exhausted, I made the impulsive decision to stop. I hadn't slept in a decent bed since Edinburgh. And the little stash of money I'd hoarded for the fishing was obviously not going to be of any use for that purpose now.

"The hotel was built out of that brooding, dark gray stone you see in most such buildings in Scotland, its window panes gleaming as if they were scrubbed every day. A little intimidated, I was standing in the parking lot below, getting my bearings, when I heard another car round the bend and roll on up the drive. A wiry Scot of about fifty, close to my age now, climbed out of a mud-streaked old Ford and nodded curtly to me, his craggy face as expressionless as that dark gray stone. He was wearing knee-high boots—Wellingtons—and a baggy wool sweater that looked so old it might have been woven by the Druids. The butt of a cigarette dangled from his lower lip.

"Even then I was conscious of how I must have looked to him. A callow, long-haired American kid barely out of his teens.

"But his wet boots stirred some conviction in me—triggered a wild, desperate hope that he might be the fisherman he appeared to be. I had seen no river for a hundred miles—found nothing in the reading I'd done before the trip that mentioned a salmon stream in the area. He had the *look* of a fisherman, I'll leave it at that."

The speaker paused to let the words register, peered deep into the lawyer's rapt face. The older man nodded, said nothing, waited with visible anticipation for him to go on.

"And so I simply asked him, point blank, if he'd been fishing. His face remained expressionless as granite beneath his wool hat as he squinted back at me. Then he stepped to the rear of his car, unlocked the trunk, and popped it open on a gleaming slab of silver so sleek and lovely it made my gut literally ache with desire.

"He said very little more, in the next couple of minutes, answering my babbled questions with that clipped Scottish thriftiness that makes words feel like pound sterling. But the few syllables he did utter were enough to make my heart leap. *Aye, I can put you on a beat. Nay, the tackle will na be a problem.* And the clincher, *Aye, the salmon are in the river. I canna say you will catch one, but the fishing has been verra good.* The sum total of what I learned further came to nothing more than a scant few additional facts: his name was Angus, he owned the hotel, and I'd have a room for the night.

"The next morning did nothing to shake my conviction that I had stumbled into Eden. The River Kerry was fewer than twenty yards across, a trickle compared to the big, famous waters I'd gazed at yearningly a few days earlier. But I was still stringing the rod Angus had lent me when a salmon suddenly materialized in the middle of the river, hung for a frozen instant above the rolling current, and splashed down in a thunderclap of spray.

"For someone who'd grown up fishing Atlantic salmon it would probably have been routine—de rigueur on the Miramichi. To me it was the most exciting, great-God-almighty moment I had ever experienced as a fisherman.

"When I'd stilled the trembling of my fingers enough to tie on one of the half-dozen flies Angus had given me, a gorgeous purple and pink creation I learned later was an Aleutian Queen, I started casting. I fished on ineffectually for over three hours, struggling with the big, heavy rod, when the strike finally came, as I was strangely, almost preternaturally certain it must. The salmon took as the fly ended its swing and wavered for a moment fifty feet below me. A gentle bump, but unmistakable. Setting the hook awkwardly, I scrambled for position, stumbling on a rock. Somehow the fish was still there, a throbbing pulse-beat through the current, now deep in the heart of the pool. It seemed content simply to lie there sulking, and I lacked the knowledge or experience to move him. Lacked the courage too, truth be told.

"The result was a stalemate, both of us firmly anchored and unwilling to yield. Five, ten, fifteen minutes we remained like this. I know because the standoff allowed me ample time for repeated glances at my watch. I dimly realized the fish somehow had to be moved—stirred into the motion that would eventually exhaust it, but I had no experience how to trigger it. The few Michigan trout I'd managed to catch in the previous months as a fly-casting novice were minnows to this brute, tethered to me by a thin strand that felt as tenuous as gossamer in my hand. Did I dare try to stir him? Unleash that sullen force into its full fury at the end of the rod?"

The narrator paused self-consciously again, his face reddening at the overheated rhetoric, but his eyes continued to burn. Carried away himself to a place he had long since forgotten he could reach emotionally, the retired lawyer only nodded. Murmured, "Yes, I understand. Go on."

Sensing it—a connection that five minutes earlier he'd have thought impossible with the stiff, over-dressed man seated beside him—the fisherman felt the remembered experience burn still more intensely in his soul. The last trace of self-consciousness vanished as he resumed.

"It was not only my timidity, the paralysis of inexperience. It was something more—something more positive—a *savoring* of the tension that kept building with every second that fish and I remained joined. For those few minutes, as I stood gathering myself for the furious surge I knew was inevitable, I think I felt more engaged, maybe even more *alive*, than I'd ever felt before. I knew I had to goad the fish into action, try to sap its will and strength. I had no idea what I would do when it moved.

"Finally I built the nerve to induce it. My palms sweating with apprehension, I began slowly raising the rod, pricking the salmon with the hook, forcing it to turn sideways into the current. It did what I feared and expected. Yet when the surge came I was totally, helplessly unprepared. The fish exploded out of the water and instantly shot off on a searing run toward a tangle of submerged roots on the opposite shore.

"As the salmon neared the snag I panicked and put more pressure on the line than it should have been asked to bear, but somehow it held. Inches short of freedom, the fish's run was checked. It wallowed there for a moment, temporarily subdued, before settling once again into a bottom-hugging sulk.

"But this time—like a drunk who had jumped into a bullring using his coat for a cape and somehow escaped being gored—I was flush with the success of my bumbling maneuver and refused to let the fish recover. Again I prodded him, denied him time to gather strength, until he sped off on another run. This one, though, was shorter, a little less bullish, and I knew I was more in control. Suddenly what had seemed unthinkable a few minutes earlier now seemed possible. I actually had a chance to land an Atlantic salmon. The thought itself sent chills up my spine.

"The fish made another, still shorter run, found itself checked once more, and rocketed out of the water once, twice, three times in head-shaking frustration. But at the end my line remained taut and the rod tip high. It reminded me, glancing up at it—that same cool, jaunty self-assurance—of the famous photograph of FDR clenching the cigarette holder in his jaw.

"Finally I was on familiar ground. I had caught no salmon and very few trout in my young life, but I'd landed hundreds of fish. And for all his great weight, this one was performing exactly like any of them near the moment of capitulation. If the hook held, all that remained was another minute or so, one or two weak runs quickly aborted, and then the silver side turned up in exhausted defeat."

Remembering, the fisherman laughed, shook his head sardonically, and went on.

"I looked at my watch one last time, curious to see how long the battle had lasted, when suddenly the reel was screaming and the salmon was busting ass downriver toward a stretch of choppy rapids like a runaway truck without brakes. Alarmed, I fingered the line with a beginner's panic, trying to slow it, and as suddenly as the strike had come the big fish was gone. The leader, that frail artery through which its life had flowed into my own for more than half an hour, now drifted limply in the slack water below my feet. With the certainty of death, I knew there would be no more salmon that day, nor probably, given my grad student penury, for many years to come.

"In the obsessed self-absorption of that moment, it felt like the worst day of my life. And yet somehow, even then, one of the best."

The historian cleared his throat, said nothing more. For some time the two men sat on the bench in the silent room, staring blankly at the painting. Strange emotions he hadn't felt in years, if ever, continued to course through the lawyer, feelings that left him momentarily incapable of response. That the stranger's tale had filled him with a sense of profound loss and regret was beyond his capacity for denial. What he didn't understand was why. The simple story of a lost fish. Something as trivial as that. Yet his heart was filled with sorrow and his eyes swam with suppressed tears. When the hard click of footsteps suddenly echoed down the adjacent corridor he quickly dabbed at his face with his handkerchief and looked up. The other man's wife had reentered the room, frowning and shaking her head.

"You're still *here*, Clay?" she cried, her hand punctuating the comment with a dismissive sweep toward the hung canvases. "I can't believe it. It's been nearly an hour. I've looked for you everywhere. You can't possibly be that interested in these paint—"

"I've just been resting, shooting the bull with my friend Fred here," the historian cut her off, a crooked smile crinkling his face in mild embarrassment. "I'm sorry. We were talking fishing. The time just slipped away."

The woman eyed both men skeptically, then shook her head again with a dramatic sigh that said she'd been down this road too many times to count—that once more she'd have to simply acknowledge this incomprehensible part of her husband's life, and forgive him. Glancing down at her wristwatch, she said emphatically, "We've got to leave now if we're going to make the three o'clock session. I need to be there for Linda's paper on the Medici, and you said you wanted to hear the panel discussion on the iconography of the cloister capitals in Moissac."

"Right," her husband said obediently, rising. He turned back to the older man on the bench and extended his hand. "It was good to meet you, Fred. Thanks for letting me ramble on like some dewy-eyed freshman. If you're ever out our way in Wisconsin, look me up. Maybe we could get out together on one of my favorite streams."

The lawyer stood too—watched intently as the historian fumbled in his pockets and took out his wallet, apparently searching for his card. Unsuccessful, he begged a slip of paper from his impatient wife's purse and quietly scrawled his name, phone number, and e-mail address. "Here," he said, "in case you ever need it. Good-bye."

The couple left the room so hurriedly the lawyer could only mumble his own short, muted farewell before their echoing footsteps receded down the tiled corridor, then slowly dissolved in the museum's enfolding gloom. He sat down again on the bench, his mind swimming, laboring to come to grips with the turmoil the stranger's story had loosed. A man who didn't even seem to own or carry his own card. Who had to scratch his personal information on a scrap of paper, like some street person or store clerk. And yet his story, his very *presence*, had moved him as nothing else had in years. How was it possible? Something as inconsequential as a fish. A fish the man didn't even *catch*. The whole overwrought experience, a *failure*, in the end.

Nothing in his life had prepared him to comprehend it. So rattled had he been at their parting he had not even given the man his own card—neglected that common, obligatory courtesy. The lawyer's cheeks burned with shame.

Valentine

This is a story about longing and isolation. Desperation. About the things they can lead you to do, or almost do, when they run high in your blood. It could possibly have happened anywhere. That it happened in Nebraska will surprise no one who has ever driven alone across the state in the month of July.

Maybe it goes without saying that this was some time ago, almost thirty years to be exact, back when things were simpler and a fair number of cars didn't have air conditioning, even in the withering heat of the plains. I was twenty, stationed at an air base just outside of Omaha. It's a city with more going for it than one might guess, given the state's bleak image as flyover country, but even in its hilly, leafy glades along the Missouri River it wasn't the Pacific Northwest where I'd been born and raised. Stir-crazy from too many weeks of drudge work, I vowed that a weekend leave, when it finally came, would take me as far from the base as I could get.

That it turned out to be a trout stream amazes me now almost as much as it did back then. I'd grown up fishing—spent countless days haunting the pine-shaded streams near the small café my parents owned on the Olympic peninsula. But Nebraska? From the little I'd seen or heard of the state, a trout stream seemed about as likely as one on the moon. The fly rod and vest lay at the bottom of my foot locker only because my previous posting had been in Colorado Springs.

I've never been either an assertive or a particularly gregarious person. Partly as a result, though I'd served for several months in Nebraska,

I'd come to know only a single individual well enough to ask for some local advice. His name was Dolph, and he was the head custodian in the building where I was a clerk typist. Two days before my leave began, I asked him what options were available to somebody with a free weekend and a gut-deep need for release.

No doubt because of the way I'd framed the question, or the fact that it came from a young serviceman cooped up too long on base, he leaned forward on his broom and flashed a crooked, knowing grin.

"What you got in mind?" he said, narrowing his eyes.

"Not that," I answered, shaking my head. Back then I was as randy as the base's flyboys, probably randier, given my relative dearth of action. But by release I hadn't meant one of the whorehouses downtown.

He stared at me in silence as the grin slowly dissolved on his stubbled face.

"What kind of *options* you have in mind?" he finally said.

"I'm—I'm not sure," I mumbled, suddenly adrift on a tidal wave of suppressed uncertainty and loneliness. For the first time since I'd enlisted, barely a month out of high school, I felt the bottomless depths of that dark sea.

The custodian was at least twenty years older than I was, married, with three or four kids and a pair of oppressive in-laws who lived half a block from his south Omaha house. That much I had learned from our previous, passing conversations. He was coarse and often cantankerous, but also innately kind in that gruff, matter-of-fact way of many men who work with their hands. "Well, what the hell did you do for fun back home?" he grunted. "Out there in them redwood forests where the sun never shines."

I laughed and told him that what I'd probably done the most was fish.

"Fish?" he barked back at me. "Shit, boy, there's all kinds o' fish down in the Missouri. And I know a couple o' decent bass lakes between here and Lincoln if you wanta get farther out o' town."

"Thanks," I said, shuffling my feet. "Don't take this wrong, but that's not the kind of fishing that interests me. What I want, you don't have here—fly fishing for trout."

28

"I don't know about that," he shot back, frowning.

I naturally assumed he meant he knew nothing of the sport. But in fact he was challenging my coastal condescension, the supposition that trout didn't swim in Big Red country. "I've got a friend up in the Sand Hills that eats trout," he added. "I'll call him tonight and find out where the hell he catches the damned things."

When Dolph saw me in the corridor the next morning his big, grizzled face split with a triumphant grin. "You're one lucky s.o.b., kid," he chortled. "Clint don't fish. He just eats 'em. But some guy he works with, that gives fish to him, told him where you can go out there if you wanta catch a mess of trout."

Even at that age, barely out of my teens, I'd been on enough wild-goose chases not to let my hopes soar. But that tingle in the gut you get at the prospect of fishing strange new water had obviously left its mark on my face.

"I see I've got your attention," he went on, mock saluting. "It's 'parently a little river called the Snake. Up near Valentine. That's about three hundred miles from here—five or six hours, 'pending on how fast you drive."

The details erased what little hesitation I'd had, whether they were phantom fish or not. "Where's the nearest car rental?" I responded quickly.

That this pleased and flattered him was written all over his own face. He stared back into mine for several seconds, saying nothing, sizing me up in a way I'd never seen him do before. "You don't need no rental," he said crustily. "I've got an old '68 Dodge you can use. Just fill 'er up with gas when you get back."

The car was waiting when a cab dropped me off at his house just before dawn the next morning, the keys under the mud-spattered floor mat where he said they'd be. I crept up to the front of the darkened house and slipped the bottle I'd brought between the screen and the door—a fifth of Johnny Walker Red whisky. I didn't know anyone well enough at the base to be confident they'd buy it for me—risk the stiff fine for giving alcohol to a minor—but when I finally worked up the nerve to approach the colonel's secretary, told her it was a gift for Dolph, she smiled and agreed at once.

I'm not sure how to describe the next few hours. I don't mean that something strange or complicated happened, for it was exactly the opposite. Slow, uneventful time spent cocooned in a moving car. But as I left the still-dark city and drove on into morning, the landscape gradually began to change, and my mood changed with it. The wooded hills along the Missouri gave way to flatter country—corn and soybean fields—and then to sparser, more desolate prairie with herds of cattle spread like brown and black dots under the vast, sun-blazing sky. I'd never seen anything like it—*felt* anything like it—the way it simultaneously shrank and seemed to expand my soul. I felt both diminished by all that open space and somehow larger, freer, than I'd ever felt before. Maybe the word that fits best is *ravenous*. I was hungrier, for whatever was about to come, than I could remember being. And that something in fact *was* about to come I somehow felt certain. Of the whole experience, it's that feeling which probably seems the strangest to me now, the most remote and foreign. The conviction, which I believe is known only to the young, that you're a kind of fixed point in the universe, where for a few moments or hours you don't feel like a tiny, insignificant speck at all. I've never read much literature, and almost no poetry, but somewhere I came across a line by Emily Dickinson that I've never forgotten. *Shadows hold their breath.* There were almost no shadows on that cloudless, sun-baked prairie, but that was the feeling I had—the same sense of quiet anticipation—as I drove on.

I reached Valentine a little after noon and pulled into the only café I saw. What I recall most is a friendly gray-haired waitress who called me darlin' and served me the first chicken-fried steak I ever ate. It was as simple a meal as I'd ever tasted, and one of the best. In the way of the rural Midwest, the portion was huge, but after wolfing it down I briefly considered ordering one more.

It was the even more ravenous hunger to fish that pushed me on. Following the scribbled directions Dolph had left for me, I headed south out of town on a narrow strip of shimmering blacktop that snaked through the arid, sand-pocked prairie grass. But there was no sign of the

Snake—no sign of *any* conceivable trout stream, for that matter. A few miles out of Valentine I'd crossed a sluggish stream called the Niobrara, but its muddy, overheated water could have harbored little more than catfish and carp.

Still, I had Dolph's word and scrap of paper, and I kept driving. A few miles farther on the terrain to my right plunged abruptly downward into an unseen canyon, and if there truly was a trout stream anywhere in the region I figured this had to be it. Pulling off on the shoulder, I switched off the ignition and stepped out into the searing heat. There was not a house in sight, any mark of human habitation. Aside from the relentless prairie wind, the only sounds were the buzz of grasshoppers and the distant bellowing of cows. Not having seen any No Trespassing signs, I grabbed my rod and vest and straddled the barbed wire fenceline—loped on across the barren scruff toward what I still hoped might turn out to be a trout stream.

I heard it before I saw it. The steep descent into the canyon was something else I'd never experienced—a stumbling, sliding drop through ponderosa pines, clusters of sumac, and sandy, ankle-deep blowouts that left me gasping from the effort and the heat. But with every step down it became clearer that the faint roar in my ears was not the wind soughing through the trees, as I'd feared, but the fall of a swift-flowing river. It's a cliché to say your heart leaps, but mine did at my first view of the Snake.

Over the next five hours I fished with an intensity, a hunger, unknown to me before or since. Part of it was the mood I still carried from the long drive through the Sand Hills and that appetite-whetting meal in the restaurant—from the boring months I'd spent cooped up on the base. But it was also the river itself. I think any avid angler can identify with at least this—the thrill of fishing new, wildly different water. And almost everything about the Snake held this mystique for me: its sandy bottom; the mercurial shifting of its currents; and most bizarrely, the sets of weird, sandstone or limestone ledges that lay barely an inch or two below the surface of the stream. I'd never seen anything remotely like them, those ledges, and I soon learned to watch acutely for their sudden presence, after a very close call. Five minutes after stringing my rod, I was splashing upstream along the shoreline with my eyes fixed on a rising trout when I came within a half-step of plunging off into roiling currents well over my head.

The river held occasional pools that looked even deeper—nine or ten feet deep, from all appearances—and I fished them intently. But it was those subsurface shelves that continued to captivate me. They held the danger and promise of huge fish lurking back in the shadows where the dark currents swept beneath.

At first I was so keen to catch a trout—*any* trout, after more than a year devoid of fly fishing—that I couldn't resist the sporadic rises I saw in the shallower water and tied on a yellow grasshopper imitation to match the activity in the shoreline grass. But after an hour or so of catching ten-inch browns and rainbows I yielded to the growing urge to go deep. Fishing under the ledges and through the pools over the next several hours, I didn't catch the monster I coveted, but I landed too many trout to count. Near the end of the afternoon I kept three or four fat rainbows, planning to pick up some ice in Valentine and give them to Dolph back at the base.

I quit fishing only because, in my obsession to get on the water, I'd neglected to bring anything to drink. By five in the afternoon my throat was so parched I had trouble swallowing. Despite all the fish I'd caught, I remained in the grip of that ravening thirst I still can neither explain nor articulate, and for several minutes I was on the verge of dropping to my knees and lapping straight from the Snake. I resisted only because I'd once known a guy who'd contracted amoebic dysentery, and wanted no part of what he'd described.

By the time I'd climbed back up out of the canyon I was close to hallucinating from the heat and thirst. That will probably seem an exaggeration, but even now I believe it to be true. All I could think of when I reached the caldron-like interior of the car was finding a house or a stock tank and begging whoever might lay claim to it for a drink.

I didn't remember passing either one on the road out of Valentine so I kept on driving in the same direction, away from town, to the south. I don't know how far I drove. You drive until you see something, anything, that lifts your foot off the gas.

On that day it was a farmhouse, set at least a half-mile off the highway, down a rutted lane that crossed over a rusted cattle guard. I wasn't sure the house was even occupied, it looked so remote and desolate across that arid prairie. But I was beyond the point of making a fully rational decision. Creeping off the blacktop, I turned into the lane as the old Dodge bounced and jarred beneath me on its worn shocks.

A few cows lay in the scant patch of shade offered by a dead, barkless cottonwood as I rolled slowly past them, swishing their tails against hordes of flies. A black bull stood nearby, his distended balls dangling grotesquely low over the parched grass. Dazed by thirst and the sun's glare, I crept to a stop a few hundred yards farther on, in front of the ramshackle old house.

Back then, during the farm crisis of the '80s, before all but the most efficient small farms vanished from the country, I suppose you saw quite a few places like it, at least in that part of America. But I'd never seen anything like it, and despite the dry swelling in my throat the look of the place was almost enough to make me turn the car around and flee.

An ancient pickup sat on rotting wooden blocks to my right, strips of gray rubber that had once been its tires dangling below the axles. Its windows were shattered. The jagged teeth of some outworn piece of machinery and tangles of rusty wire poked up through the scraggly weeds.

I finally switched off the ignition but remained there, peering through the windshield at the house. A worn pair of cowboy boots had been shucked off on the doorstep, spattered with thick flecks of mud or cow shit. Peeling paint curdled under the porch eaves. Upstairs, I thought a sun-bleached curtain stirred faintly behind a narrow window, but it might simply have been my eyes filming in the glare. There were no cats or chickens, critters you'd expect around such a place—not even a mangy dog, which would have calmed me a little even if it had been hostile. The only sign of life was the soft cooing of a pigeon from the shadows in the rickety barn.

I don't know why all of it, even the murmur of that pigeon, spooked me so. There was no rational reason. Maybe that's the point. All I can say is that what I felt in those couple of minutes went beyond anxiety. It was something close to visceral fear, and it only got stronger as I continued to sit there, peering through the dust-caked windshield at that old house closed up like a fist.

It seems absurd to me now, in retrospect, what my mind conjured up in those moments. Lampshades made of skin. Severed heads in a well. Corpses strung like slaughtered cattle behind the door of the storm cellar. I said something to myself, out loud, just to break the silence. Finally I took a deep breath and climbed out of the car, walked slowly up to the house.

I stood on the step for another long moment before knocking, bent closer to peer through the fly-specked screen. When my eyes adjusted to the glare I could make out a few things inside the porch: old newspaper pages covered with dirt-crusted onions; a hooded gray sweatshirt on a wall hook; some crushed beer cans beside a sagging, broken-backed chair. The signs of human occupation calmed me a little, and taking another deep breath I leaned back and rapped lightly on the door. When no one answered I knocked again, louder. Still there was no response. Despite my thirst I was so relieved I exhaled audibly—turned and took a few steps back toward the safety of the car.

A door creaked suddenly on its hinges behind me, and I sprang around in alarm, my gut quivering with dread. Still I could see nothing but the shadowed screen of the porch. Then came another creak of the inside door, and a couple of slow, shuffling footsteps across the floor.

Several moments more of silence passed before I saw her. An old woman stood just inside the screen, peering out at me. She appeared to be wearing some type of thin white or gray bathrobe, but through the dark mesh I couldn't tell for sure.

"Yes?" she murmured barely audibly. Then, louder, "What is it?"

"Excuse me, ma'am," I blurted. "I'm awful sorry to bother you." Even as I said it I was aware of how phony the words must have sounded— reflexive grease, like "Have a nice day," though I don't think that expression was common currency in America back then. Embarrassed, I took a step closer and tried to be more honest, told her I'd been fishing the Snake all afternoon and had neglected to bring any water—paused again when she didn't respond and shuffled my feet awkwardly, finally asked if she could give me a drink.

Through all of this she remained back in the porch shadows peering dubiously out at me through the screen. But after five or ten more seconds of silence she took a step forward, where I could see her better— saw that she wasn't old at all but quite young, a woman not much older than I was. The jolt was so disorienting I didn't catch her response and she had to repeat it. "Come in," she said softly, opening the door.

I followed her across the creaking boards of the porch into the kitchen, where a slash of late-afternoon sunlight knifed between the parted curtains of a west window—cut a swath of illumination across the dark room's worn linoleum floor. As she stepped through it I glimpsed the curve of her buttocks beneath the thin cloth of her bathrobe, the wet sheen of her thick black hair. That I had roused her out of an upstairs bath seemed obvious, as unmistakable now as the stir of the faded curtain that had made my heart flutter with dread five minutes before.

It fluttered again, as I stood there staring at her. Neither of us said a word as she reached up and lifted a Mason jar off a cupboard shelf, stepped back through the patch of sunlight and filled it to the brim with tap water from the sink. Even then, all those years ago, I thought of it as I still do now—one of the kindest things anyone had ever done for me. In the same circumstances, almost anyone else would have simply filled a drinking glass.

When she turned to hand the jar to me—stepped a final time into that slash of sunlight—my eyes dropped and through the damp garment I glimpsed the dark, heartbreaking wedge between her thighs.

I don't know if she noticed this, recognized the flood of emotion that was washing through me. Lust. Trust. Immense gratitude and longing. I looked away in embarrassment and for the first time noticed the smear of spilled coffee across the yellowed linoleum in the corner— the shards of a shattered cup and still-wet stain down the cracked panel below the sink. The cup had been thrown, not dropped. There was no other logical conclusion.

Given what happened in the next few seconds I assume she must have seen that observation register on my face, but it's a question I'll carry with me as long as I live. I know only that when she handed me the jar the air had become charged between us—that her eyes stared into mine with a look my gut recognized as something close to my own unexpressed emotion, and that they brimmed with tears. Still neither of us spoke. Finally I managed a thank you and took the jar from her—felt its cold seep through the glass into my hand. "Thanks—" I repeated even more clumsily, not knowing what to call a woman who was so obviously no longer a "ma'am."

"My name's Jack," I mumbled. "What's yours?"

"Rachel."

For another few seconds we remained there, staring at each other in that silent kitchen where a stack of dirty dishes and a strip of peeling wallpaper loomed garishly behind her right arm.

"You're not from around here, are you?" she said finally.

"No . . . I'm from Washington . . . Washington State."

"It must be really beautiful there," she responded, looking away.

What more she might have said—perhaps wanted to say—if I hadn't been so tongue-tied is one of those unknowable things you find your thoughts drifting back to for years after. I was so far from being able to express what flooded my own heart I might as well have been mute. I knew nothing about her, her life or her situation—the tight-jawed rancher I took to be her husband who passed me five minutes later in his battered pickup as I drove numbly down that long lane on my way back out to the road. All I knew was that my chest was full of mad desire to snatch her hand and pull her away with me, away to whatever the future might hold. Instead, I did nothing. Simply lifted the jar and began drinking until the water washed away the dryness in my throat and spattered down across my T-shirt. I drank until I started coughing, until there was no drop left in the quart jar and the spillage wet my shoetops—drank until she burst out laughing and I did too, breaking the tension in the room.

At least the outward tension. My head continued to swim with images of that shattered cup, the tears in her eyes, and I still burned to know her—to ask her about her life out there in a place most people would think of as the end of the world. Instead I blurted, "You're terrific, Rachel," let my eyes hold on hers as my fingertips brushed self-consciously across her shoulder—felt still the coolness of her flesh beneath the thin cloth as I walked out into that blinding, late-afternoon sun.

The Conception

The boy could smell the pines before he saw them. Or he thought he could. Cramped in the back seat between the sweating thighs of his older brothers, he caught only glimpses of the dark jagged line rising out of the miles of plain still ahead of them—said nothing of what had swelled for minutes in his chest. That smell, and what it meant. *The Black Hills.* Even a year earlier, his first time, the scent had started something vibrating inside him before he had any idea of its source.

When he could no longer contain his excitement, no one else in the packed, overheated car understood. His teenage brothers jabbed his ribs and mocked him. His father simply teased.

"I can smell 'em from here, Scotty. Can't you?"

"Don't kid him, Harold. You know how upset he can get."

"Look! Now I can even *see through* 'em. Just below that ridge, under the cloud cover. See it—*the water*? Those fat rainbows swimming around in your favorite pool?"

Hoots of laughter and more jabs from his brothers. A quick shushing groan from his mother, looking back nervously into his eyes until she felt sure he wasn't going to gouge or kick out at their legs.

Thirty years later, when memory has sloughed away so much else, the fisherman can call up those moments—the smell of the pines, the acute anticipation—as if it were yesterday. Approaching a trout stream, he felt more than a trace of them still. He had never been poetic or philosophical enough to fathom why this should be so. Why his father and brothers had seemed to look forward to that annual week of August

38

vacation as much as he did, but never fished—just stared vacantly at his catches, interested only in their appearance an hour later on the cabin's dinner table. Why they'd teased him mercilessly the morning he'd blurted, "You've ruined the whole day!" after no one had wakened him at dawn so he could spend every daylight hour on the stream. Somehow in a bipolar universe the gods had ordained fixed sets of opposites: man and woman, death and life, those who lived to fish and the far greater number who did not. He rarely went deeper into it than that.

What he found himself doing instead as he settled into middle age was simply *remember*, and inevitably with the remembrance, *compare*. It was not the kind of thing he had ever shared with another fisherman, though he fished with many, nor to these comparisons too did he attach any great philosophical weight. His mind channeled down a flow of embedded images that laced rocks and runs and shaded pools together across half a lifetime of fishing North American trout streams, a kind of angler's déjà vu. A month earlier, wading round a bend on the San Juan, he'd stood transfixed for several moments trying to remember where . . . where . . . until it struck him. *The riffle on the Wenaha in eastern Oregon where he'd caught a dozen good browns on an Elk Hair Caddis the morning he'd sprained his ankle on the rocky trail down.*

A river of linked images, widening with every year. Now more than three decades had passed since that first cradling of a fly rod in his small hand. It had all begun back there, on Spearfish Creek. South Dakota. A ten-year-old boy thrilled beyond measure by this unconceived world of pine woods and burbling clear water only a few hours' drive from his home on the other Dakota plain.

That first rod was made for casting bait, no doubt bought over the counter from a hardware store in Minot. A Christmas or birthday gift chosen by his uncomprehending but indulgent dad. For sure, the reel was a retractable, heavy as a rock with its fascinating bead-tipped metal tongue. Nearly everything else, from those annual late-summer vacations, had sloughed away from the swell of memory like dry skin. Even the name of the girl from California in the next cabin he'd had the mad crush on when he was fifteen. Yet almost everything about the *fishing*— that still seemed almost as vibrant as it was then.

Each night before bedtime, creeping along the wet grass on the clipped lawn in front of the cabins, tugging half-emerged night crawlers out of their holes while his flashlight beams down from his other hand. Bending to splash the last cobwebs of sleep out of his eyes, stepping into the stream at dawn, the frigid water chilling his right foot through a pinhole leak in his waders. His fingers trembling with the cold and eagerness as he threads the first crawler on the Eagle Claw and bites the split shot closed with his teeth.

The trout were small. Browns and an occasional rainbow no longer than a foot, nearly all of them stocked from a hatchery truck out of Spearfish. In those eight years of family vacations, before he went out east to college, he remembers only a single individual fish. But he remembers it with the same keenness that flows across the decades whenever he smells a Ponderosa pine.

A few years earlier, driving I-90 cross-country to Seattle, he had pulled impulsively off in Rapid City and retraced their old route back through Deadwood, Cheyenne Crossing, and Savoy. Much of it had changed scarcely at all. Several of the same names remained word-burned on varnished shingles, hanging over the plank bridges to the owners' log cottages across the creek. But the lodge where his family always stayed was gone, as was even the faintest trace of any cabins. He knew he'd found the site only by the stone bridge and the rocky pool beneath it, unmistakable from the countless boyhood hours he'd spent swinging his bait up into the shadows under its abutments—letting it drift down until the current popped the crawler or salmon egg cluster to the surface a few yards below his feet.

How often had he glanced up to find the lodge manager watching him through the office window, a grin creasing his tanned, movie-idol face? Once—he must have been eleven or twelve by then—the face had turned away in a mock, Olympian exaggeration of reproof.

Had the manager's gentle jibing begun then, or even earlier? All he could recall now with any certainty were the words the manager had said to him as the bottle of salmon eggs slid across the glass counter into his grubby hand.

"You're still using these, Scotty? The tips of your fingers are going to get stained permanently. They'll be red as raspberries for the rest of your life."

A long pause had followed, the boy and man grinning familiarly at each other. Then, "See this pretty little thing? It's called a Royal Coachman. It leaves your fingertips clean as a manicure when you tie it on."

Another smile follows the tease, but somehow less familiar, then a wink of the eye beneath the slick jet black hair that makes the manager's perfect teeth look even whiter in the tanned, chiseled jaw.

The fisherman had just enough reflection to wonder now, remembering it, why the flame had burned so brightly and instantaneously from that moment. He had kept on drowning night crawlers and dunking salmon eggs for a couple of hours after he'd shuffled out of the office. But early that evening, while the manager's new bride took his place behind the counter, the boy had sloshed eagerly downstream toward that favorite pool under the bridge and been brought up short to see another fisherman standing in the riffle below it. In the moment his heart sank it also filled with envy and wonder. For it was Bill. Bill Wilson, the manager, casting something too light and small to see. Was it that Royal Coachman? The boy had no way of knowing. Could only stand there in the stream and marvel at the line's long fluid arcs through the evening air.

His own wadered feet had splashed to an abrupt stop just short of the bridge, very near the point where the downwash would have spooked any rising trout for twenty yards below it. The look on the manager's unsmiling face was something else that had often flashed back to him on occupied stretches of water in the years since. *Don't take another step*, it said. *Tonight, this pool is mine.*

How many trout had his silent mentor caught in the minutes that followed, the boy holding there rapt above the bridge, watching him? Six or eight? A dozen? However many there were, all but two went back into the water—one more thing, like the lovely fly, that back then was as foreign to him as the monks of Tibet. Whatever he managed to catch himself on all those worms and eggs, he kept, occasionally even stuffing one or two deep into his waders if he was over the limit. Everyone in his family loved to eat them. And he struggled so hard to hook and land the few he did somehow tease into striking that any guilt he felt came only after the euphoria had ebbed slightly, long after he'd thwacked the wriggling fish on a rock and sneaked it down along his pants leg below his canvas creel.

41

Would the flame have caught a year or two earlier, if he'd come upon the manager fly fishing then? No. Almost certainly no. He wouldn't have been ready. Green wood burns in a roaring fire, but it doesn't kindle. And just as certainly, it took a Bill Wilson to kindle his. Someone else would have done it eventually, some lesser god, but at that age, on the cusp of adolescence, only a man he had lionized from the first moment he'd seen him could have shaken his addiction to catching trout by whatever means he could.

Not for the first time, the fisherman tried to recapture how the lodge manager had appeared to him back then—the evening of that boyhood epiphany:

In the winter, a ski instructor at a place called Aspen in Colorado. Tall, with hair like Steve McGarrett on Hawaii Five-O *and sunglasses dangling on a cord below his jaw. Married sometime in the previous year to a beautiful icy blonde who his mother had told them over dinner earlier in the week (the family all ears) was a former Braniff stewardess from Chicago. Able to get out on the water now only because the marriage had briefly released him from his usual evening chores assigning tables and attending to the richer guests who ate their dinners in the lodge restaurant across the lawn from their larger cabins next to the stream.*

He bored deeper into the memory, trying to recall the cabins' names—both those bigger, more luxurious ones beside the water and those his own family and other poorer families rented that were set back deeper in the pines:

Potato Creek Johnny. Calamity Jane. Wild Bill. The expensive cars parked outside their fully furnished units bearing license plates from Massachusetts and Texas and New York. A world away from Preacher Smith, the cramped cabin his family always stayed in, with its creaking hand pump for their drinking water and the too-small woodstove to heat the chill Black Hills nights.

Back then, he could not have cared less about the privation. Yet from the moment he'd stood agape at the manager's ivory line unfurling in the day's last glittering shards of sunlight—seen the sudden bulge where a split second earlier the unseen fly had feathered down—he had cared like hell.

Yet that wasn't the individual fish he remembered. Out of whatever number the manager had gone on to catch that evening, and the fifty or a hundred the boy himself had caught, all of them on bait, in those years just short of adolescence, the fish he remembered was the one he had caught the next morning. Had kept and triumphantly cleaned with trembling fingers on the stream bank. Toted on a full run, stumbling in his waders, back to Preacher Smith bursting in on his still sleeping family shouting "*Look! Look!* I caught this on a *fly!*"

The fisherman stood now below a pine-shaded pool on one of the best steelhead rivers in British Columbia, where the clean, faintly antiseptic scent of the trees and something in the rocky curve of the shoreline have pulled him back to that joyous moment in his youth. The memory triggered a burst of laughter audible enough the angler above him turned abruptly and stared at him across fifty yards of stream.

The laughter had swelled in his throat at the still vivid image of the ragtag fly he'd used, and the way he had fished it, and, most of all, at an undersized child's fanatical will. Closing his eyes as the laughter died, he stood at the foot of the blue-ribbon pool much as he'd stood at dawn below that stone bridge half a lifetime earlier, tying on the only fly a boy's enflamed desire had been able to procure.

Dazzled by the manager's skill and success, he had sloshed back to the cabin for dinner with the flowing furls of fly line still lancing through his brain. He was too shy to enter the lodge office where the chilly wife stood behind the counter. Too intimidated to have approached her, mumble that he'd like to buy a fly. In any event, he'd had no money, even if he could have stiffened his backbone—would have had to bear his brothers' ridicule by asking his dad.

The prospect was as far beyond his reach at that moment as the languid curls of line that had flowed minutes earlier from the springy rod in his mentor's right hand. Yet a few days before—the evening they'd checked in—while he was lying on the floor tugging on his too-tight waders as the precious daylight dissolved in the west, he had glimpsed a tiny patch of blue and crimson pinned above the cabin's doorframe. It was made of feathers. There seemed to be a scruffy pair of what looked like wings. It had to be a fly.

Remembering it, the fisherman burst out laughing once more— barely managed to stifle it lest the upriver angler hear him again and scuttle away to call the nearest mental ward. Garish as the brightest Atlantic salmon tie in creation, an imitation of no aquatic or terrestrial creature that ever lived on earth, the tatter-winged concoction had almost certainly been made in Japan or Korea. Hookless, it might have come from a dowager's hat, or been snatched off the G-string of some honky-tonk stripper. But it *had* a hook, strong enough to prick deep and forever the life of a callow child.

It was a trout fly. In those feverish hours, that was more than enough.

Sometime after supper, unnoticed by either his brothers or his parents, he hops up on a chair and snatches it down.

On his canvas cot that night, his stream-chilled legs warming in his sleeping bag, the boy lay awake far longer than usual as his charged brain teemed with images and pipe dreams: the curls of line flowing from the manager's long fingers, fish after fish caught and released in a matter of minutes, his own chances of finding a trout innocent or dumb enough to strike at the tuft of feathers drifting by its nose. Yet as he approached the stream at daybreak that next morning, the dew still icy on the grass beneath his feet, hope briefly soared through the doubt and anxiety weighing his chest. His rod remained strung from his abrupt stop the previous evening, a shriveled, rock-hard night crawler still attached to the hook.

It took him several minutes to remove it. And at least that much longer to bite off the Eagle Claw, remove the precious tuft of feathers from the tiny aspirin tin where he had secreted it, and tie it on with his fumbling hands. He'd left the split shot on the leader. This too the mature fisherman recalled with acute clarity. Finally he was ready. Of the several hundred thousand casts he has made and hopes still to make in a life shaped by the love of fishing, none is launched with more nervous anticipation than that first ever cast with a fly when he was not yet thirteen.

And of course like nearly all such casts, in angling or life or work that strives toward art, absolutely nothing happened. The weighted leader sank deep into the pool and emerged at the bottom end hung up on a rock.

Disappointed but not daunted, the boy tugs the fly free and casts again. And again. And then so many more agains a water nymph abiding in the glassy current might have lost count of them. And still he casts. For he knows the trout are there, the fly sliding past them. He has seen them often in the high afternoon sunlight, a dozen or more finning slowly down in the depths.

An hour later he was still there, casting. And at last the sun cleared the overhanging ridge behind the lodge—struck the now unshadowed water. The boy stopped for several minutes to let his eyes adjust. Finally he could see them. He was experienced enough to know from their slightly darker coloration that all but one were browns, and he began to direct his casts at that single, largest trout that looked green in the water, its lie perhaps two or three yards above his planted feet.

And now another first cast, with only slightly less anticipation than the real first almost two hours earlier. And again, nothing. But a purpose has been served, an observation made—the first and perhaps most important of many such observations destined to help him down through the years from all those childhood days spent fishing bait. He's not going deep enough. The tuft of blue and crimson has been drifting several inches above the big rainbow's nose.

He quickly bites on another split shot and casts again. And then again. Then suddenly it happens. Bored or hungry or finally enraged beyond the point of bearing a moment longer the taunts of color dancing past its snout (what fisher has ever known, even those with ages more experience, the thing that triggers a reluctant fish to strike?) the trout slides an inch to its right and the feathers disappear into the brief white gape of its maw.

Even now, remembering, jacked up since an hour before dawn as he drove with boyish anticipation toward the fabled Canadian river, the fisherman knew he had never—sadly, *would* never—have a moment to match what happened next. The rainbow felt the barb. It shot up and tail-walked across the surface of the water. *The boy lifts the rod tip instinctively and plays it up and down the pool audibly praying please God please God don't let it snap the leader or shake the hook.*

A minute or so later the fish was spent. Unsnapping his mesh net from his belt, he'd slid it giddily under the rose-streaked side and lifted it thrashing out of the water. *The thrill is so palpable he can't still his quaking fingers—is able only with concentrated effort to remove the tattered fly and take out his tape measure. Confirm the monster's length.*

Fourteen and a half inches. Three inches bigger than any trout he had ever caught before. The previous evening he had left the stream while daylight remained, the first time in those August vacations it had ever happened.

That life-changing morning was the next.

An hour later, he'd bought the first true flies of his life, a prim pair of the flame-bright Royal Coachmen. They cost sixty cents each. With the dollar his father had given him he had asked for only one, but the grinning manager had dropped a second into his palm.

"I appreciate the stream etiquette last night, Scotty. You've earned these. But fish 'em on the surface, okay?"

Another sly grin and then another gift, no less unexpected. A thin pamphlet the manager lifts off a shelf above his desk.

The angler remained at the foot of the steelhead pool, his rod rigged but idle beside him—tried to imagine what this iconic mentor would have seen as he turned back and slid the thin paperback across the counter glass into the boy's stubby hand. *A towheaded kid in a Fighting Sioux hockey cap, small for his age, the look on his freckled face a mix of insecurity and wonder and bottomless desire.*

Too intimidated to mumble more than a scant fraction of the gratitude welling inside him, he'd carried his trophies back to the family cabin. Then he did something else he couldn't have conceived a day earlier—spent the afternoon reading rather than fishing. But not just reading. Periodically, he'd risen from where he sat alone at the table by the lodge's spacious lawn—tried to imitate *The Basic Principles of Fly Casting* illustrated by the black and white penciled diagrams in the little book. By the time his mother insisted he come into the cabin for supper, he had managed to throw forward perhaps fifteen feet of line off the heavy reel past the tip of the whippy, unbalanced rod.

He'd fished from dawn to dark the next day, the family's last before returning to North Dakota, and caught three or four trout. All were on the salmon eggs that remained in his creel. He had snapped off both Coachmen before the sun had cleared the ridge. Not until the following summer did he learn the pointlessness of fishing such a gaudy attractor fly in the shadowy currents of dawn.

But he has begun. He reads, then reads some more, through the snowy depths of a prairie winter. Christmas brings the better reel and lighter rod he has pleaded for. A Fenwick. His March birthday brings a weight-forward line and a dozen hand-tied flies. They remain untouched, pristine in their plastic compartments, as his casts spread mostly longer and truer over the lawn below his upstairs bedroom and then into a muddy farm pond a half-mile from his house. Another August comes at last. When the family Buick approaches the dark line of spruce and pines on the horizon, the boy prays that he is ready. There are no eggs or night crawlers in his creel, nor, he vows, will there ever be. But he has only just begun to conceive what lies ahead.

Anglinguistics

I had a really lucky thing happen to me this morning," my wife announced from the far end of the table.

We were in the "How did your day go" beginning of dinner. "Oh yeah?" I responded half-listening, munching my salad.

She stared at me for several seconds before going on.

"I'd driven out to that orchard on the old river road. You know the one, the little farm where they sell apples. On the way back I had a flat tire."

"Some luck," I grunted.

She rolled her eyes, and finally resumed.

"So there I am, alone out on this deserted gravel road. You know how little traffic it carries. But I'd managed to get the jack out of the trunk, and even figured out how it worked."

Surprised, I stopped chewing and told her honestly I was proud of her. "A lot of women would have been helpl—" I said, before catching myself at the sharp tilt of her eyebrows. "Hell," I self-corrected, "these days, a lot of men, too."

"Obviously."

"Okay," I forged on. "So . . . okay. . . . You managed to get the spare on?"

"No. That's where the luck comes in. I had the car jacked up and was using that cross-shaped thingy to take off the love-nuts but one of them was so tight I couldn't budge it. I kept put—"

"Lug nuts," I cut her off, suppressing my own roll of the eyes.

"What?"

"They're called *lug* nuts, not love nuts. Sorry for interrupting. Thought it's something you'd probably want to know."

"Why are they called that?"

"I have no idea," I finally admitted after ten seconds of silence, groping to come up with some plausible explanation as my brain went as dead as the air. Whatever shred remained of my macho quotient had taken another direct hit.

"I don't know," she said, eyeing me dubiously. "*Love nuts* never made any sense to me, I'll admit it, but with men you never know. I thought something about their size or the way they were shaped probably explained it. In your minds at least. Some weird guy th—"

"Okay, I get the picture," I cut her off again. "Let's get back to this lucky break you say you caught. What happened next?"

She took a long sip from her wine glass before going on.

"I was really frustrated at that point, had no idea what I was going to do. But then I heard a kind of clattering sound and this old black pickup rolled around the bend and slowed down as it came on toward me. It pulled off on the shoulder and rattled to a stop."

So did my wife. I'd briefly looked away as she spoke, picked up my salad fork, and resumed munching. A bad move.

"Sorry," I said, swallowing. "I'm all ears. Go on."

Her lips tightened but I knew they couldn't have fallen silent at that point of the story if I'd ignored her completely and grazed the table clean.

"Well, this old man with long flowing white hair climbed out," she continued, "holding a cane in his big gnarly hand. Not a cane exactly, but some kind of carved stick, like a staff. He was old but tall, and straight as a soldier. He stood there peering at me through his wire-rimmed glasses, still clutching that staff in his hand. I was really scared."

"My God," I said, startled, a faint twinge of foreboding already rising in my gut. "But things turned out okay in the end?"

"Better than okay. He was on his way into town—simply stopped to see if I needed any help, which I obviously did. It took him only a few minutes to get the tire off and put the spare on. He was amazingly vigorous. Everything about him looked, you know, so weathered and *hard*, but he was actually a very nice old man."

"You never know," I murmured, relieved.

She looked down and took a slow nibble of her own salad, and I resumed munching as well, thought she was finished. When she spoke again her voice had changed—taken on that slightly forced, airy lightness that makes a man's heart sink like a stone.

"You're probably not going to like the next part," she said, glancing coyly at me.

I didn't say anything, simply waited, knew the "probably" was sure to be a monumental understatement. The way she'd described the old codger—his "hard" appearance and the "staff"—continued to stir the foreboding in my soul.

"He didn't say much the whole time he was helping me," she went on, "but I think his voice was the most distinctive voice I've ever heard. It sounded kind of Scandinavian, but really archaic, like he'd stepped out of some old Bergman movie. And . . . I'm not sure how to describe it. . . . It was kind of . . . kind of *biblical*, I guess you'd say."

Each word, every pause, hit me like the thud of a hammer. The foreboding grew until it pressed like an anvil on my chest. I'd said nothing more, listening to her, but my discomfort had become so obvious she dropped her fork and stared bewilderedly into my face.

"What's *wrong*, Ernie?" she blurted. "I haven't even told you the part I said you probably weren't going to like."

"*Bunderson*," I rasped under my breath.

"What?"

"*Bunderson!*" I repeated through clenched teeth. "*Moses!* That's gotta be the guy that helped you out."

"You *know* him?" she said, her eyes widening. "Yes, Mr. Bunderson—that is what he called himself, though I thought he said his first name was 'Gund,' not 'Moses.' 'Gund H.,' actually. I remember because he—"

"We *call* him Moses," I waved her dispiritedly to a stop, not wanting to know anything more. A few years earlier I'd spent the longest four hours of my life duck hunting with him. It was like the Bataan Death March telescoped into a single morning. On the river, Moses was as legendary and about as popular with other hunters as the bubonic plague.

"That's even luckier then," she resumed brightly. "Since you already know him it won't be a problem, setting the outing up and everything. You can simply give him a call tonight and arrange your day togeth—"

"*What!*" I cried, lurching out of my chair.

"Calm *down*," she said, raising a palm. "It's only a few hours. I know you prefer to fish by yourself, and I've dreaded telling you all afternoon. But what choice did I have? I mean, he'd gone out of his way to help me. And he absolutely refused to take any money for it. So when he put the jack back in the trunk and noticed one of your fishing rods—asked me if it were mine . . . well, . . . what could I do? He was clearly so *interested*, and one thing led to another . . . I mean, I didn't have any *other* way to express my appreciation to him!"

Her eyes narrowed like I'd implicitly asked her to do something unspeakable, the words hanging in the air like grim death.

But by then I'd almost stopped listening, the bitter memory of that duck hunt still flooding my brain.

Dawn broke over the willows as I staggered panting up to his blind behind him. Assuming we would set them out together, I dropped the two sacks of weighted decoys he'd left for me to carry down the long, brushy trail from the road. Instead, he stood on the shore in the dim light with that crooked staff in his hand, pointing to the reedy edgewater where he told me to spread the stool.

"Rejoice, O young man in thy youth," he croaked as I struggled to drag his decoy boat down a gravel bar into the river. "Hasten to thy labors. Unseemly the ways of the slothful man."

Twenty minutes later I was towing the emptied boat back toward his blind. Moses stood rigid as a statue beside it, the staff replaced by a long-barreled twelve-gauge in his hoary hand. Suddenly he dropped to his knees and shouted, "Kneel! Kneel in the water!" The command was so urgent I instinctively dropped as if poleaxed—stayed crouched as a stream of ice water lipped the top of my waders and trickled down my left leg. At about the same moment I caught the flash of flaring wings and heard his double-barrel belch a single volley. A drake mallard splashed down in the river, twenty yards past the decoys. In the current's heavy chop it began to drift swiftly away downstream.

"Hasten thy feet!" he shouted at me, waving his arms imperiously. "Rejoice for the suppleness of thy limbs!"

By the time I retrieved the duck and wallowed back to the blind, my lungs burned like a furnace. I said as much to the old coot as he plucked the duck from my shaking fingers and dropped it into his sack.

"Happy the man of vigor," he croaked, tossing the sack into the blind.

"I've got a bootful of water," I barked back at him. "My feet are frozen. And I've yet to chamber a shell in my gun."

He refilled his pipe, bent slowly, and lifted another bag off the sand. "Woes without number are visited on the improvident man," he grumbled, handing me a pair of dry socks.

Okay," I shook the memory away and turned a hangdog face back to my wife, surrendering. There was no way around it, short of fleeing the country. But if I had to take the old codger fishing, I was damned if I was going to go out with him again alone.

"I'm bringing a couple of other guys with us," I added. "Might as well share the wealth."

"Who?" she replied instantly, her eyebrows tilting with suspicion.

"You don't know them," I mumbled. "Just a couple of dudes I met at work. They've been bugging me to take them out ever since they got here. One of them's from England and the other's from France. They ought to get along with Moses real well."

Whether they would or wouldn't I didn't know, and didn't care. A drowning man doesn't do background checks before climbing on a life raft. All I knew was that I needed to put as big a buffer between myself and Moses as I could get, and the two foreigners were my best bet. None of my regular hunting or fishing buddies was going to get within a country mile of him. What the hell, I even managed to assuage my conscience, the three of them might actually hit it off together. There were circus acts, after all, with a dog and a cat and a mouse.

The sun was peeking through the woods behind Moses's log house when I pulled up beside his rattletrap pickup a couple of days later. He was standing impatiently on his stoop holding a bamboo rod and a wicker creel, his other hand clutched tightly around the staff. White hair billowed beneath his felt hat in the morning breeze. A worn pair of hip waders, black-patched too many times to count, cloaked his aged limbs.

"Sorry I'm a little late," I mumbled, climbing out of the car. "I stopped on the way out of town to pick us up some coffee and a few donuts."

He eyed me silently through the wire-rimmed glasses as I dropped the old rod and creel in the trunk. Inside the car, he took the cup of coffee from the holder and snatched a pair of donuts from the box. His craggy face resembled a block of weathered stone.

"A pearl in a swine's snout," he barked between bites, "the glory of the dawn to the sluggard in his bed."

Neither of us said anything more for several minutes as I drove on toward my other riders—the pair I hadn't yet mentioned to him. Moses didn't seem to remember me—recall that we'd once shared those grim hours in his blind together—and I figured silence was golden. Several years had passed since that outing, and my hair was noticeably thinner. I even had a different car.

We'd rolled another mile or so up the road when the booming bass sounded again.

"Thou hast waxen fat since last we sojourned," he said sharply, opening the box on the seat and plucking out the last of the donuts. "Weighty the flesh on thy loins."

I stared at him hard, biting my tongue. That single morning in the blind had been more than enough to convince me that his rants were best left unanswered. Better simply to change the subject—offer him a grudging thanks for the aid he'd given my wife.

"Good of you to stop and help Brenda," I finally calmed down enough to mumble. "Hard for her to change a tire by herself."

The old man took a long sip from his coffee cup and peered at me through his glasses, a tiny crinkle flickering in the crow's feet around his piercing blue eyes.

"A comely woman," he responded. "Rejoice in the suppleness of her limbs."

"I do," I spluttered, spilling what was left of my own coffee. It didn't seem like there was a hell of a lot more to say.

I won't describe the next half-hour. Suffice it to say that five minutes after I'd picked up Jean-Claude and "the Admiral," as the portly Englishman liked to call himself, I had my circus act all right, but not the one I'd idiotically hoped. The saving grace was that the crucial part of my plan had worked. Between them, the pair of foreigners gave me so much buffer Moses barely acknowledged my presence by the time we reached the stream. They occupied so much of his steely attention, in fact, and he theirs, that the unimaginable eventually happened. I actually began to enjoy myself.

The best pool for a mile up or down Beaver Creek flowed beneath a streamside weeping willow thirty yards from where I parked the car. Moses's eyes gleamed like Christmas lights when he saw it. Already wadered, he grabbed his gear and was calf-deep, probing its lower end with his staff before Jean-Claude and the Admiral had shed their shoes.

The Frenchman had taken off his pants and was standing in his blue bikini briefs, about to pull on his neoprenes, when the old man's voice boomed at him over the water. "In the name of God, sirrah, cloak thy gaudy buttocks! Like unto a bull's pizzle, the private parts of the shameless man!"

"What is ze matter with him, monsieur?" the Frenchman turned to me. "I think *peut-être* he is crazy in ze head, no?"

"Not a bit of it, old sport," the Admiral barked beside him, huffing into his own chest waders. "You aren't proper, eh? It's frightfully indecent. Grant the old fellow his due."

The Frenchman swore something under his breath and finished changing. When both of them were ready I led them up the trail skirting Moses's pool, where dimpled rises broke the surface in front of him like falling rain.

Now it was the Englishman's turn for irritation.

"Am I given to understand," he said to me sharply, "that your hoary friend has proprietary license to that beat?" His eyes were locked on the coveted water, where a fat rainbow was already tail-walking at the business end of Moses's rod.

"He's not my friend," I shot back at him. "But, yes, he was the first to claim it. The beat goes on."

The Frenchman laughed sardonically. The Admiral glared at him but held his tongue.

We walked on upstream another hundred yards or so, to a lesser stretch of water I thought should be big enough for both of them. The Frenchman was about half the Admiral's age, and quickly claimed the preferred flow on the opposite shore. Seething like his chin whiskers were on fire, the Englishman marched into the stream too. For the next twenty minutes I sat on the bank watching the two of them conduct a kind of angling thrust and parry, their rods moving grimly over the water like fencers' foils. Finally, despite their mutual flogging of the surface, the Admiral somehow managed to hook a small fish.

The fly was barely removed from its mouth before he turned to his tight-lipped companion.

"Just takes a bit of the old bob and tickle, laddybuck," he crowed at him. "Keep your pecker up. Every dog has his day."

Jean-Claude said nothing, the muscle tightening visibly on his lean jaw.

Ten minutes later his rod bent suddenly and it was clear that this was a bigger fish, if only marginally. "Ah, yes, *mon ami*," he cackled at the Admiral. "Ze dog has barked, *oui*? *Peut-être* you would like to know ze fly zat I am using—ze one zat has given me *la bonne chance*?"

"Not a bit of it, Clod," the Admiral fired back. "We *invented* fly fishing. I came to manhood on the Test."

"Zat may be, monsieur," the Parisian responded, hoisting the twelve-inch brown like a champagne flute toward the sky. "But it is ze Frenchman who has invented making ze amour to a beautiful woman. Zat is ze true *test*. And what is fly fishing but making amour to ze fish?"

Once again I didn't catch all of what the Englishman muttered through his beard. Part of it was "Wanker" and "Sod off."

Neither of them managed to hook anything more in another half-hour of slapping the water, their stabbing casts finally reaching such a crescendo of pique and frustration the dumbest carp on the planet would have been put down.

I followed as they trudged back downstream toward Moses's pool, where the old man still stood. He'd moved less than twenty yards in the time we'd been gone. We watched as he hooked another rising trout with a tiny white fly that dropped on the water like a snowflake. Even from a distance it was clear his creel was heavy. He released the fifteen-inch brown with a deft flick of his gnarled hand.

It was more than the Admiral could bear. Stomping on down the trail until he stood facing him, he shouted at Moses across the water, his words as sharp as his florid face was red.

"You commandeered the only prime reach on the stream!" his voice echoed. "I shouldn't wonder if you've brought twenty fish or more to hand!"

Moses stepped onto the grass and laid down his rod, slowly refilled his pipe, and took a long puff.

"If a bear happen upon a honeypot," he intoned, "bountifully is he blessed."

This time I could hear every profane word the Admiral shouted. So, obviously, could Moses.

"A dog to his vomit," he barked sternly, "curse words to the man of wrath."

So how did it go?" my wife asked tentatively when I stepped into the house an hour later. She was smiling hopefully, but it was clear she was prepared for the worst.

I stepped past her to the refrigerator and pulled out a cold beer—took several swigs as long and deep as Moses's pipe inhalations.

"A fox in the henhouse," I said, smiling at her, "the quiet man among backbiters of neighing tongue."

Spanish Fly

C all me Pedro."
    The words seemed innocent enough at the time, merely the latest of his harmless quirks, like his taste for flamenco music and the occasional pitcher of sangria. But they loom now, looking back, as Pete Smith's private Niagara—the moment he went over the edge.

When I fished with him next, a month later, he was working an evening midge hatch on the Madison. He'd pulled his hair back into a tight ponytail. A new pair of black neoprenes stretched over his rawbone frame, sheathing it like a body condom. And the dinged canteen that had bounced against his lean flanks for years had been replaced by a goatskin bota.

"What the hell's got into him?" Clyde croaked that night as we sat hunched over our tying vises in his den. "The bastard looks like he just got off a bus from Juarez."

I didn't respond, intent on palmering a webby length of hackle over a dyed tuft of fur from a roadkilled coyote. "Beats me," I finally mumbled, still locked in on the streamer emerging under my jittery fingers. The shape and color of a stick of dynamite, it was destined to hit the water as the Big Wile E.

"A shrink would have a field day with that guy," I added, snipping off a wayward guard hair. "He's getting weirder all the time."

Wally nodded and slid off his stool. "I need another brew," he said, heading for the kitchen.

Clyde squinted at his disappearing back. *"Cerveza,"* he growled, his arthritic digits bent around a hot-pink swatch of woodchuck ear hair. "Bring me one of 'em too."

"Serve you what?" Wally said, turning back. His oval face furrowed in the blue light of the refrigerator door.

"Another beer," I said. "Disregard the Clydester. Whatever bug bit Pete must have got a piece of him too."

"Are you nuts?" Clyde shot back. "I was just repeatin' the only word I've heard from him lately where I had some idea what he was sayin'. What the hell's a taco bar, anyway?"

The old electrician shook his head in disgust. Hanks of fur sprouted like centipede legs from under his thumb, fringing the hook he'd wrapped with elastic from one of his ex-wife's garter belts. Over the years I'd seen him tie the gaudy fly by the boxful, swearing he'd quit tying them the day he extracted one from a fish's lip. The bibulous night of his divorce, when he'd created it, he'd christened it the Over 'n Dun.

"*Tapas* bar," I corrected him. "It's a bar that serves appetizer-type food. He told me they're big in Spain, like all the other stuff he's gotten into since he came back from that vacation. You've heard him. *Huevos rancheros. Paella.* Classical guitar."

Clyde's baggy eyes rolled toward the ceiling as the tying thread snapped under his thumbnail.

"Far as I'm concerned, it's all a bunch of bull," he groaned.

"That too," Wally said, handing him his beer.

A few weeks later the four of us were out again, on bigger water, and the season had changed. The aspens had turned golden and the cottonwoods had begun to drop their leaves in the gunmetal runs and the riffles that shimmered like silver in the autumn breeze. Pete leaped out of the van before the motor died and scuttled off into the pines, a leather saddlebag slung over his rod case. The raven hair he hadn't cut for months fell in long raffish strands down his shoulders. His nostrils flared like a rutting deer's.

When he strode out of the trees ten minutes later, he carried his fly rod like a lance and wore a small wedge-shaped hat that crowned the braided ponytail. An embroidered vest rode stiffly over his shirt, open above a thin black tie that made his lean frame look even thinner. Or maybe he *was* thinner, it was hard to tell.

"God almighty," Clyde puffed, pulling on his waders beside me. "What the hell's he gone and done now?"

It took some time before I could answer.

"I don't know," I finally said, mesmerized. "He's been reading a lot lately, I know that. I saw him come out of the public library when I drove past it last weekend. He had about a dozen books in his arms."

"Goddamn," the electrician repeated, grinding the butt of his cigar into the sand. "When I first met him, he sold bathroom fixtures. And most of the fish he caught were on a Number Three Mepps."

"He still sells bathroom fixtures," I said. "They're just more upscale. He found some company that imports painted ceramic toilet bowls from Madrid."

"That's prob'ly why he's so damned skinny. He ain't sellin' enough of 'em to eat."

Slowly donning my own gear, I watched as Pete strode past with his eyes narrowed, his belly flat, and his dark face creased and tight like a walnut's skin. The face worried me until I looked at it closer and then it worried me more.

Wally shambled up beside us, his eyes bulging like a carp's. The three of us watched as Pete entered the river. He splashed on past a gravel bar where any of us would have stopped to cast into the riffle above it, slowing his pace only when the deepening folds of water began to lap hard and threateningly against his thighs. Leaning into the current for balance, he fumbled for his new fly box, thin as a cigarette case inside the pocket of his spangled vest. His privates bulged like a ballet dancer's. The new neoprenes glinted black in the sun.

A fly somehow appeared in his hand as the surging current swept him several yards downstream—spun him through a funnel of whitewater as he turned in a pair of twinkling pirouettes around his rod. But he didn't go down.

"How did he do that?" Wally's awed voice whispered beside me. "Holy God!"

"He's always had great balance," I murmured. "But that was world class for sure."

We stared even more intently as he knotted on the fly, trying to guess what pattern he'd selected. Pete's eyes narrowed further as they moved over the water, reading its bumps and bulges. The one thing I was certain of was that there couldn't have been many flies left to choose from the once-encyclopedic rows that filled his old fly boxes. A week earlier, through a sweaty night in his cramped bachelor apartment, he'd pared down his collection with the zeal of a weight-shedding wrestler, discarding both flies and the books where he'd learned how to tie them. Everything published after the advent of Flashabou had been jettisoned around midnight. He'd apparently come to some kind of closure around five in the morning over the broken spines of Swisher and Richards, his bookshelves bare now of all but Art Flick.

"Whaddaya think he's goin' with?" Wally nudged me in the rib cage. "Nothin's rising, and if he ain't lyin' he's chucked most of his nymphs and all of his attractors and streamers. I still don't have a clue why."

"He got rid of anything he thought was 'tricked-up,'" I said. "*Trucos*, he called them. He told me every time he opened his box and saw them staring back at him, it felt like he'd opened the door of a cheap hotel room and seen something lewd."

"So what's he got left?" the mailman mumbled, shaking his head.

"Not much," I answered. "A few mayfly imitations. One or two Cowdungs. At least one Royal Coachman I know he's got stashed away."

"I still don't get it," he said, his round eyes blinking behind his glasses. "The Coachman's about as gaudy as a fly gets. It's gotta be one of them *trucos*."

"You're right," I admitted. "But when I picked him up this morning he dug it out of the kitchen trash can just before he closed the door. I almost couldn't watch him. The grimace on his face reminded me of a man falling off the wagon, reaching for a fifth of scotch."

Wally pulled out his handkerchief and blew his nose.

"I guess it's not all that surprisin', if you think about it," he said. "When he was just getting started the Coachman was the only fly he ever used."

"It was the fly that hooked him," I said, nodding at the memory. "I suppose it's about as close as feathers come to a red-and-white Mepps."

We continued to watch. Clyde clumped back up the bank past us, stopped, and stared out at him too, then shook his head and disappeared around the bend.

Pete had inched out even farther into the river. It humped and thrust at his loins as he arched his back, stripped line, and began casting toward an upstream eddy. A shadow fell across the water. Banks of clouds were rolling in from the mountains, sealing off the sun.

"If we're gonna do any fishing ourselves, we better get goin'," Wally murmured. "Look at that sky."

A half-hour later we were still watching Pete, the rods idle in our hands. He hadn't had a strike and no fish were working and the freshening wind had blurred our eyes and put a steady drip in Wally's nose. It was Pete's casting that held us—the beauty of his rod painting the water in a dance of feathery kisses and curls. He made long casts. Wind cheaters. Switch pickups and negative curves. And then, still fishless, he began to blanket the river with casts I knew only because one night, when I'd driven by and seen him in the alley behind his apartment practicing in the moonlight, I sneaked into his room and checked the book that lay open on his desk.

The rhythms of his rod had come straight from their yellowed pages—fired them into art as we watched. His casts flowed so hypnotically I heard my lips murmur the reverent words he'd been whispering when I'd left his room that night and crept up behind him in the moonlight—a eulogy to "Mr. Charles Ritz of Paris France" who "threw a bow so tight" the faded photographs hit you "like a *cornada* cut through the heart."

Wally and I remained on the shore watching him, our eyes fogged with wonder. Wally's rod was trembling in his hand.

Finally Pete hooked a fish. It was a small fish, no more than twelve inches, but it was a thick-shouldered brown and it fought bravely and it came to hand with bright speckled sides glinting in a thin patch of sun. Pete arched over the rod, motionless, his back ramrod straight and his legs together. He released the trout with a single deft flick of the barbless hook, then turned abruptly away from the wild river's roar.

Bouncing joyously out of the run, he splashed back across the gravel bar, his vest and tie dripping, to a patch of brush near where we stood. The bota hung where he'd left it, looped over a willow. Hoisting it above his head, he squeezed a spurt of red wine toward his open throat and bit it off savagely as a few droplets sluiced down his chin.

Wally wiped his nose with the back of his hand, took a wary step backward. Pete's eyes looked like a pair of white marbles that had just been glazed in a kiln.

None of us said anything for some time.

"Man, oh man," Wally finally ventured. "That was awesome. You're doin' stuff out there I've never seen."

Pete said nothing. He hung the goatskin back on the willow. He turned slowly and stared out at the current bulging darkly under the lowering sky.

"The maximum of exposure," he murmured. "The purity of line."

He stepped again into the river.

This time he waded even farther out than before. The current beat now against his rib cage. Coils of line unfurled on the little patch of slack water his straining body had created behind him as he stripped them off his reel.

A light snow had begun to sift out of the sky, flecking the warp of his wool hat, but the noiseless casts again shot long and true across the wind-whipped water. The fly landed daintily at the top of the run, just above a large boulder. Below it, the current split into a pair of deep chutes that funneled menacingly back together where he stood twenty yards below.

My hands had stiffened from the fear and the cold but I remained watching, following the orange fly line as it licked over the river like a tongue of flame. He used to be a little quick, I thought, remembering the old Pete. Was still just a shade limp-wristed. Or maybe it was envy. The strides he'd made since I'd last seen him fish were as astonishing as the hat and spangled vest he wore. Somehow, it all began to fit. I was no aficionado, but to my watering eyes each cast looked cleaner than the one that preceded it. The arcing rod seemed to bend the brawling river to its will.

Behind me, I heard Clyde stumble up to join us. He was gasping, whether from the exertion of hauling his girth up the sandy bank or from the spectacle riveting his own snow-fringed orbs I wasn't sure. Pete had edged out two or three feet farther—stood now on his toes, casting to the glassy lie behind the boulder. His taut frame loomed through the thickening snow like an apparition glimpsed through a veil.

On the third cast he appeared to roll a fish, but he hooked nothing. Ten minutes later he again stood beside us on the shore.

"By God, that's a big one," he crowed. "Big *bicho*. He's holding in his *querencia*. I can't get him to work." Lighting a cigarette, he took two or three short stabbing puffs before flicking it disdainfully into the river. The butt spun downstream past him as he splashed again out over the bar. Clyde stared at his departing back, muttered something I didn't catch as he headed for the Bronco. Wally and I stayed where we were, peering through the snow.

"He *is* nuts," Wally said. "Clyde's right. The dude's about three aces shy of a full deck."

Staring numbly at his rod, he began to break it down. "But I got to say this for him," he added. "He's damn sure been gettin' something out of all them books he reads. Makes me think I shouldn't of dropped out of school."

I didn't get out with Pete again until the next season, after the spring runoff had spent itself and the water had cleared enough you could glimpse pebbles on the river floor. I'd seen him a few times during the winter, mostly through the ice-glazed window of his apartment, bent so intently over his desk I didn't feel inclined to stop and break his focus. I did look up the word *querencia* in a Spanish dictionary. Learned it's the part of a bullring where a bull returns after engaging the matador, the place where it feels most safe.

When we finally did make it out on the river, Wally came too, despite the fact he had to call in sick at the post office to do it. Clyde grumbled like hell, said there was no way he'd go out again with the crazy bastard, but I knew in the end he'd be waiting on his porch with his thermos of Irish coffee and his battered rod case.

I had volunteered to drive, to pick Pete up at dawn, hoping the few minutes alone with him driving across town would give me a jump on the questions we all had about his latest aspirations. The first answer wasn't long in coming. "What river do you want to fish?" I asked as we idled at a stoplight, peering out at the first faint pink streaks in the sky.

He slowly turned from the window at the words, jolted out of some private reverie, a thin smile creasing his face. Shaking a cigarette out of his crumpled pack, he stared at it for a long moment before lighting it, finally responding in syllables so soft and distant they hung like the cigarette's smoke in the air.

"There is but one, amigo," he murmured. "The rest are *nada*. Today we fish the Bighorn."

A couple of hours later Wally and I stood on the big river's south bank with our rods strung. This time Clyde remained with us, waiting. He'd muttered under his breath, rolled his eyes whenever Pete's name came up over the winter, but we all knew the odds he'd strike off downstream and miss whatever was about to happen were roughly the same as his coming up with another garter belt from his ex-wife. If anything, he looked even more expectant than Wally, whose tales of what he'd missed the last time had turned more than one of our winter tying sessions into a concert of bearish grunts and growls.

Pete had directed us to a private ranch that flanked the river—a roaring stretch where the river, charged with spring snowmelt, tumbled down through a gauntlet of fire-blackened pines. A ring of scorched hills formed a kind of moonscape behind it. The short grass shone black as a sable pelt in the morning sun.

Already ponytailed, Pete climbed out and again toted his gear into a changing place behind a rock. When he reemerged, it was clear his winter pilgrimage had led him through a lot more library shrines.

Still, the red neoprenes and peacock-bright vest surprised us less than the flies. He'd left the wafer-thin box by his rod when he disappeared behind the rock, and Wally had snapped the lid open before Pete's ponytail vanished from view. The collection had been pared even further. It held now only a single pattern, a trim hairwing I knew the name of only because he'd delivered a paean to it that morning as we drove through the dawn-lit streets. He called it the *Papa Wulff.* Told me it was "a hybrid." Said he'd created it as a legacy to the two *toros bravos* whose streamside memories would "rise forever in the sun."

None of the half-dozen flies was larger than a mosquito. A step into the river, he tied on the tiniest and spat on it for luck.

We watched as he moved out to where the current darted hard at his knees.

When the first cast came even Clyde could see it was flawless, and I heard him gasp behind me as the tiny fly moved over the water and dropped with the purity of a communion wafer forty feet from where we stood. Then the line lifted and sang again through a set of backcasts that swelled into a kind of symphony, the new rod gleaming like a baton in the morning light. Clyde took a lurching step forward, bumping my elbow. Wally's right hand rose in a sun-shielding salute above his eyes.

And then Pete moved farther out. A lot farther. Far enough that the bludgeoning current suddenly bounced him downriver in a heart-stopping surge that miraculously ended with his feet somehow secure behind a foam-caked rock. The Bighorn roared on into the whitewater chute a few yards below him. My own heart was thumping like the river in my throat.

"Jesus," Wally croaked. "Jesus God."

Clyde glanced at him but said nothing. The color had drained from his face.

We watched as the casts began again, rose and slightly accelerated, spread over the river like a fan. Casts so chaste they made you forget the danger and the fire-ravaged prairie and even the raging river that gored at Pete's groin. His left leg was slightly advanced, taut as an arrow, his right a shaft of sinew behind it. The rod kept lifting and then lifting as the ivory line scrolled lyric parabolas out of his hand.

When the strike came he set the hook gently, almost indolently, and played the fish off the reel. It was a fine fish and he played it fine and cleanly as it bullied up and down in heavy surges that ended only when he released it with a quick, barely perceptible flourish of his left wrist. The rod curved above him as he executed the release, the bow of his body a mirror of his arched right arm.

Jubilant, he bounced out of the river to the collective burst of our pent-up breath, each step punctuated by our gasps of foreboding. Wally was cradling the bota as he reached us, and he snatched it from the dazzled mailman's trembling fingers the moment his foot struck the shore. The jet of wine hit the back of his throat an instant later. He bit it off with the finality of a steel door slamming in a jail cell. Swallowing hard, he wiped the sweat from his eyes, then lifted the goatskin again and gulped several more hard mouthfuls before spitting the last on the sand.

"That was incredible," Wally whispered.

The fisherman stared back at him, faintly smiling.

"*Cojónes,*" he murmured. "*Grandes huevos.* I tell you, amigos. That fish had balls."

None of us responded. Clyde pawed a trickle of tobacco juice off his grizzled chin.

Then before we could reach out to him Pete stepped back into the river—plunged farther out, pirouetting on his toes as the current bumped and shouldered his bony frame toward the very throat of the narrows. I looked away as a wave of nausea washed over me. But again his feet somehow caught—found purchase on the churning gravel bottom. When my eyes opened on Pete again he stood chest-deep in the lee of a flood-stacked cluster of logs that had hung up on a rock. Its jutting edge rose out of the river like the prow of a ship whose shattered spars marked the violent water for several hundred yards below.

Wally had dropped to his knees. I fought off the nausea and fixed my eyes on a charred hill in the distance, where the prairie fire had burned itself out. Clyde stood at my other elbow, his jaw clenched around the butt of his cigar.

When I looked back at Pete, somewhere in the fusion of fly line and blinding sunlight a trout shot out of the river in a tiara of spray. Pete set the hook and played it—played it off the reel whose hum I could faintly hear over the roar of the river and the sudden hiss from the gravelly throat at my side.

"*Olé!*"

Stunned, I turned as the big trout soared, saw Clyde's cigar butt drop on the sand as his gravelly voice cut the air again with the ferocity of a chainsaw.

"Olé! Olé!"

And suddenly the tears were coursing down my cheeks as Wally rose to his feet and his choked voice swelled to join Clyde's and my own in a full-throated cry over the raging stream.

"Olé! Olé! Olé!"

Pete turned, glanced toward us at the sound, the rod trembling in his hand and a grin splitting his face like the beatific smile of an angel. And in that nick of a second the big fish surged and the river hooked Pete's thigh and a few stunned eye blinks later he was gone.

We found his body a half-mile downstream, grappled by a tangle of roots, floating in a quiet pool below a grassy bank that hung low over the shaded water. Strangely, there wasn't a mark on him. He still clutched the shattered rod in his hand.

Rage

They had come off the water an hour earlier still fuming.

"Those goddamned sonsabitches," the realtor swore. "I'd have coldcocked that motherfucker driving if we could have chased him down."

The doctor said nothing, bit back the remains of his own anger with another salty sip from his margarita. It was watery and diluted, as warm and nondescript as the seedy Texas bar where the two of them sat.

"It's not often conditions are that perfect," he answered finally. "Tide coming in. Nervous water. Gulls diving everywhere and fish feeding less than twenty yards away. I'd dropped my fly just off the nose of one of the two or three biggest I've ever seen when that first wake-wave washed in."

"Those goddamned motherfuckers."

The doctor lived in San Antonio, fished the coastal saltwater flats half a dozen times every season. The realtor, from San Francisco, had never fished for redfish before.

"We'll try them again tomorrow," the doctor said, unconvincingly. His brother-in-law was scheduled to fly home later in the afternoon and the morning tide wasn't promising. But that fact he didn't mention. Best not to make him any angrier than he already was.

"You never know, on public water," he said instead.

"I've always hated those fuckin' things," the realtor spat, unmollified. "Boats are bad enough, but at least they need a couple of feet of water. Those damned Jet Skis can go anywhere."

"I've never seen one before on that flat."

"Well, you've seen one now. And five'll get you ten you're gonna see the bastards there again."

Neither of the fishermen said anything more for some time—pushed what remained of the stale drinks aside as the realtor ordered another round. The cowboy-booted waitress silently delivered the fresh ones and carted the rejects away on a metal tray.

"I actually did coldcock a guy once on the Deschutes," the realtor said, his eyes lingering on her body as the young woman walked out of the bar into the attached restaurant. "I was on a kickass steelhead pool, one of the best on the river. Cocksucker moved in on me so tight I'd have hooked him with a backcast if he hadn't called me a selfish asshole, got up in my face, and made me nail him first with my fist."

The doctor stared across the table at him, expressionless.

"It happens," he said softly, sipping his fresh drink.

The first time the two men had met, the day before his wedding six years before, the physician had realized within five minutes that they had and would almost certainly never have anything in common but fly fishing. Up to now, it had been enough. He'd discreetly tried for several minutes to steer the conversation away from the incident on the water, had the same success he'd had trying to fathom the realtor's redneck politics.

"So does shit."

He looked at his brother-in-law again, thought what the hell. If they weren't going to let go of it, so be it. At least the story was relevant. The guy was his wife's brother, after all, hard as that was at the moment to take.

"The one I remember happened about ten years ago, on the Bighorn," he began. "I know you've never fished it. But you know all about drift boats. And in the fifteen miles or so below Yellowtail Dam it's how most guys out there are fishing, the majority with a guide."

The realtor stared back across the table, noncommittal. Something in his own face or tone had abruptly raised the ante, the doctor recognized—left the disgruntled in-law visibly wary of what was to come. Taking another sip of the margarita, he tried to soften whatever edge his words held.

"No big deal, if you fish there enough and know the conventions. But occasionally you see some friction between the drift boats and fishermen who are wading, usually when the latter are working a hatch alongshore.

"Most of the time it's nothing more than a long glare, maybe a few words muttered under the breath. Rarely does it rise even to the level where insults are exchanged. I think it would happen more often if the guides weren't as good as most of them are."

Still the realtor said nothing, took a swallow of his own drink, but held his tongue.

"But the incident I'm about to describe got a lot worse than anything I've ever seen, before or since.

"As I said, this was several years ago, the first time I'd ever fished the river. I was with a med school buddy from Colorado and we hired a guide out of a fly shop in Fort Smith, the little burg by the dam. He was young, even younger than we were, and came from somewhere back east, someplace in New England, as I remember. But he knew his stuff. He'd fished the Bighorn for two or three summers before he started guiding on it, and it showed. In the first couple of hours the two of us probably caught fifteen or twenty trout.

"We'd taken all of them on Sowbugs and San Juan worms, just off the bottom. Nothing much was happening on the surface. Then, around noon, we came to an island that split the river down the middle, and we could all see as we got closer that fish were working a hatch in the shallow channel to the right. High bright sky, less than two feet of water. A stretch where it would have been awfully easy to put every one of those rising trout down as we approached. But here too the kid showed how good he was. It took both strength and savvy to maneuver the drift boat outside them—wrench it into the deeper current along the south bank and then swing us back upstream to a gravel bar twenty yards below the nearest rise. It was a caddis hatch, that was immediately clear to all three of us, and a few of the rise forms we'd seen as the boat skirted the riffle were big enough to put your heart in your throat."

The doctor paused, remembering, took another swallow from his drink as his brother-in-law waited edgily for him to go on. The realtor—a man far more accustomed to talking than to listening—sat across the table with the tight, sullen expression that marks a face when impatience and curiosity conflict.

"The channel was narrow enough there was no way to get the boat below them without putting those larger trout down," the physician continued. "But there were still enough scattered rises we were all confident that if we simply waited a few minutes, stayed out of the river, the bigger ones would resume feeding too. None of us had eaten since breakfast, and it was close to lunchtime. So we sat down by the boat and took out our sandwiches and beer.

"I suppose we'd sat there for ten or fifteen minutes, munching and getting increasingly pumped as the water started to boil again with rises, when a pickup rolled up on the south bank and parked there, no more than fifty yards away. The doors opened and two little kids jumped out. Indian kids, the older a girl maybe six or seven years old. The other was a little boy holding a pink plastic ball. Before their parents even emerged the kids were tossing and kicking it back and forth up the shore.

"I should probably have mentioned earlier that this part of the Bighorn, the prime part, flows through the Crow Indian Reservation. It's open to outsiders only because of a Supreme Court ruling several decades ago, a case the Crow had appealed unsuccessfully all the way up the chain. So it's fair to say there's always a little implicit tension, though I've fished the river several times the last few years, occasionally just walking the shoreline, and run into Indian fishermen without any problem—even had brief but outwardly friendly conversations with two or three."

The realtor grunted dubiously, the first sound he'd made since the narrative began. But still he said nothing, sat drumming his fingers on the table waiting for the doctor to go on.

"The mother was attractive, we could all see that from across the channel. She appeared to be about thirty, attentive to the two kids but also to her husband, who'd pulled a spinning rod out of the back of the pickup and begun running a small silver lure through the deeper seam of water the guide had swung our boat through a few minutes before. He was close to six feet tall, sinewy, wore jeans and a light blue work shirt. His hair was that glossy, stunning black you see in full-blooded Indians, tied in a ponytail halfway down his back.

"All three of us sat staring at them. But I didn't sense any real friction. He wasn't casting into the riffle where the fish were rising, and we had no designs on his run. When we looked back at the water above us and saw that the bigger trout had begun feeding again, in fact, I almost forgot the Indians were there.

"And then something happened I've never seen again on the Bighorn, or anywhere else, for that matter. Something that changed everything in less than the time it took to put every one of those rising fish down for good.

"My friend and I had each tied on an Elk Hair Caddis—were about to enter the river—when a raft hove into view a hundred yards or more above us, plenty far enough above for the pair of fishermen to see us— see that we were fishing dries and choose the other side of the island to pass by. But as they got nearer it became clear—sickeningly clear—that this wasn't going to happen. They were either going to float right through us or along the bank where the Indian was casting his lure.

"Our guide was already on his feet, shouting and waving them toward the other channel. And for a few seconds I thought he might have succeeded—saw the guy in the stern, working the oars, try to jack the thing around and head it that way. But it was too late. The guide could probably have done it, but even he'd have had his hands full, given the kind of craft it was. A big keelless rubber inflatable that looked far more like a life raft than any drift boat you've ever seen."

Again the physician paused, shaking his head at the memory. His brother-in-law was a skilled and experienced enough trout fisherman the story's now apparent climax finally moved him—roused at least the vicarious recognition any angler feels at another's soaring hopes suddenly gone up in smoke.

"Stupid motherfuckers," he muttered. "You should've all taken out your knives and put about a dozen holes in the fuckin' thing."

"It's possible what happened next wouldn't have escalated to the point it did if my friend and I hadn't made our preferences clear when we got on the drift boat that morning," the doctor continued, blocking out the comment and the hostility that flared in the other man's glowering face. "But we'd both told the guide we wanted to fish dries whenever it was possible, and for four hours he'd kept his eyes peeled for exactly the kind of surface action we'd found. So when these two knuckleheads in the raft drifted through, he flat lost it. As I mentioned, he was young, volatile—probably saw the size of his tip shrinking with every fish the raft sent scurrying for cover. And it put down all of them. I was enraged myself—didn't say anything mostly because the guide was filling the air with so many curses any more would have been superfluous. But there was also the obvious fact that the guy rowing didn't have a clue what he was doing—had so little control of that big overinflated thing it spun around in a complete circle as they approached. Which only pissed the guide off even more.

"By now they were directly in front of us, ass-backward in the current, and over the guide's stream of curses I thought I heard the guy at the oars start to apologize. It was too late, regardless. There's virtually no chance anything he said would have made any difference. The guide was so furious by that point he was literally screaming at them, 'You stupid assholes! Get off this river! Are you too fucking blind to see it's our piece of water? You're too incompetent to be within a thousand miles of this place!'"

"Damned right," the realtor muttered. "I'd have said the same fuckin' thing—and prob'ly coldcocked that numb-nuts with the oars."

This time his brother-in-law paused for so long, staring across the table at him, the realtor's face colored, then turned hard.

"What?" he barked defensively. "Idiots like that *don't* belong on trout water, let alone on a blue-ribbon stream."

The doctor appeared about to respond, but said nothing, picked up the narrative only after he'd taken another long swallow of his drink.

"For the first time since the raft appeared, I looked across the river. The two Indian children had stopped chasing their ball and stood on the shore gaping at us. *Listening* to us. Their mother had her hand on the little boy's shoulder. The father had apparently set the spinning rod on the ground—it was no longer in his hand, at any rate—and he stood staring across the river at all of us too. His eyes, even at that distance, burned like coals in the mask of suppressed anger that was his face.

"My own eyes were now locked on the four of them, so I didn't really see, only heard, what was happening closer to me—the fisherman in the bow of the raft screaming back at the guide with his own stream of curses—cries of 'This is our fucking river as much as yours!' and 'Shove it up your fucking ass!'

"I kept staring at the Indians. Saw the mother's fingers tighten on the little boy's shoulder, her other hand reach out and draw her daughter closer to her side. The father glanced back at them as she did it, then turned again to glare at us across the channel. The raft had spun on past us, downriver, when the guy in the bow started laughing. A hard, cynical laugh that was harder to take than his curses and insults had been a few seconds before. I glanced back at the raft at that point. Just before it drifted out of sight around the tip of the island, the guy raised his rod and did a set of tomahawk chops with its butt end. His voice rose over the river in a kind of up and down wailing he clearly wanted us to take as a mock Indian war chant.

"The guide was still screaming at him, giving him the finger. I turned away to look again at the Indians. The woman had herded the kids back into the pickup but the man hadn't moved—still stood there glaring at us across the water. It was impossible not to think of defeat, humiliation—and of Pyrrhic victory, the famous battlefield less than an hour's drive away across the plains. The Crow had been scouts for Custer. I thought of all of it as I stood there, staring back at him, my anger draining away into feelings of complicity, of shame."

The doctor's eyes dropped awkwardly to his half-filled glass, the drink gone watery and stale as his first. He had said far more than he intended. Revealed far more of himself to a man who remained a stranger than he would have imagined possible an hour before.

Across the wooden table the realtor looked just as uncomfortable—turned abruptly away and began signaling aggressively toward the restaurant.

"Time to hit the road," the doctor said, forcing a smile. "The women will be waiting."

"Fuck, yes. We've sat here way too long. Where the fuck is that girl, anyways?"

The Devil's Arse

The state isn't important, nor is the year or the name of the river. Say simply that the celebrated water I had driven halfway across America to fish is in the West, the time was several years ago, and the river's trico hatches in recent years had become so famed they'd begun to draw insufferable hordes of anglers every August. I'd fished it for a decade, remembered the way it once was. I doubt that I would otherwise have paid the slightest attention to the gravelly voice from across the dimly lit room.

"Nobody ever used them damned things in my day."

The place was one of those all-purpose little haunts you still occasionally find in the outback, selling gas, beer, and cheap tourist curios in grime-streaked glass cases that hold even a few staples for desperate fly fishers. I'd stopped to gas up and pee—bought the dusty packet of strike indicators only because of a moment's uncertainty whether I'd noticed any in my vest when I packed for the trip a couple of days before. The grouchy old-timer had said nothing until I paid the girl behind the counter, slipped the packet into my shirt.

"A man don't need 'em if he watches his line and can recognize a strike."

He was seventy-five or eighty, spidery, his knuckles bulging like marbles below the frayed cuffs of his too-large sweatshirt. A beer bottle was clutched in his hand like a weapon. I glanced at the girl as she handed me my change. She smiled knowingly, gave a sardonic roll of her eyes.

I should have ignored him and walked out the door. But something in his eyes, the way they glinted at me behind the wisps of gray hair, got under my skin.

"You don't look like a man who can recognize much of anything anymore," I said.

It was an insult I instantly regretted, however accurate it might have been. I am not by nature a combative person. In the icy silence that filled the room, my embarrassment was strong enough I turned abruptly back to the girl and ordered a pair of beers.

The geezer said nothing as I carried them to his table in the corner—set one down by the empty he still clutched in his bony hand.

"Look, man," I said, dropping into the chair across from him. "I'm sorry. You probably know a lot about fishing in these parts."

"You can bet your sorry ass I do," he hissed, the rheumy eyes boring into my face.

I don't know how long I sat there in the gloom, sipping the beer, staring at him across the pock-marked table. I don't know why I sat there. His eyes held me, that's all I can say, as did his voice when at last he spoke again. Maybe it was the beer I'd brought him, or the genuine remorse he saw in my face, or simply the fact I remained there so long even an angry, lonely old man softened a little. Whatever it was, he proceeded to tell me about a place so mesmerizing I couldn't have risen from the chair if I'd wanted to—a piece of water that set the blood pounding in my chest.

He said that he could count on his hands the number of fishermen who knew about it—tally on one those who had ever walked it holding a rod. Yet it was less than thirty miles from where we sat talking, no more than an hour from the blue-ribbon river I and so many other anglers came to fish every year.

He said he once caught a dozen trout over five pounds out of its waters in a single afternoon, two of them ten pounds or larger. Finally, when I asked him what the place was called, his lips curled over his tobacco-stained teeth as he paused, narrowed his eyes demonically, and croaked, *"The Devil's Arse."*

It was such a ludicrous name I burst out laughing—a spontaneous expression of the disbelief I'd long since come to hold for the whole far-fetched tale. His glinting eyes narrowed at the sound and his voice hardened—became again the venomous rasp I'd heard earlier when I paid the girl. She had vanished into the rear of the store. No one else had entered. Once again I apologized to him and stood to leave.

"This country was settled by an Englishman, a hunnert and fifty-odd years ago," he muttered. "It's what he named the canyon—that part of the river—you dumb sonofabitch."

He drained the last dregs of the second beer I'd bought him and clattered up out of his chair too—muttered one thing more.

"He died out there. It's one of the reasons nobody fishes it. But I fished it, more than once. And I'd fish the damn place again if I could."

He spat on the floor and hobbled on across it past me. It was my first look at his legs. One of them wore a prosthesis, stuffed into a scuffed leather boot.

I left the rented cabin before dawn the next morning and was on the river I'd crossed the country to fish not long after sunrise. The stretch of water I headed for was close to two miles upstream from the end of the road. I'd discovered it several years earlier—a narrow, glassy side channel the drift boats usually neglected. It was also far enough from any public access that few other anglers reached it on foot. When the hatches were on, the fishing could be beatific. Some of the most pleasurable hours I'd ever spent holding a fly rod had come on this little scrap of water, barely fifty yards long and a few paces wide. Whimsically, a couple of years earlier, I'd christened it *Heaven's Neck*. I had never seen anyone fishing on it, a stroke of luck or grace I knew someday had to end yet remained seductive enough to nurse the kind of denial only a lovesick illusion can spawn.

It ended with a jolt that knotted my stomach. Every year— whenever I emerged from the streamside patch of willows where the Neck first hove into view—my throat swelled with that mix of dread and anticipation familiar to any angler with an antisocial bent. The stocky young fisherman who glared down the channel at me clearly shared this temperament. We stood facing each other, the current breaking hard around his waders. The stripped fly line that coiled on the slack water behind him gleamed like a hangman's noose in the early morning sun.

I caught some fish in the next few hours, nymphing my way dispiritedly back downriver. But I was determined to rise even earlier the next morning—be on the grassy bank beside the Neck long before the first trout broke the surface of the warming stream. You can imagine my emotional state, then, when I tell you that the same bearish frame glowered at me over the steaming river when I stepped out of the frost-fringed willows at dawn. The expression this time on his pink face fused contempt with proprietary triumph. I stared at him the way you stare at the trailing end of your leader after the biggest trout you've ever hooked has broken off—those hollow seconds when the sense of loss registers in full. Then I retraced my steps back down the river without stringing the rod in my hand.

I thought of little else on that long walk to my car but the grizzled old-timer and the mythic water with which he had taunted me. For that is exactly how his croaky voice echoed in my memory—a taunt—as if he were *daring* me to fish the place. Maybe if I'd reached the Neck that morning and found no one there, or if there hadn't been so many drift boats gliding past me on that disheartened trudge downriver, or if the only other stretch of stream I thought might be unoccupied hadn't been choked with four novices using plastic strike indicators the size and color of tangerines . . . maybe if even one of these facts had been different I would still be fishing—fishing the way I once fished—but who's to say? I can swear only that I finally succumbed to his story, the demonic glint in his eyes.

The directions he'd given me were unerring. A gravel road branching north off the highway, a jog west to a steer skull nailed above a failed and abandoned ranch's entrance, then another turn back north through a sand-drifted cattle guard to the canyon rim. By the end the wheel ruts I was following were barely perceptible. I climbed out of the dust-caked car and trotted avidly past it to peer down over the dropoff—felt my pulse race at the glinting seam of water splitting the lush valley far below. The narrow trail down didn't appear severe, but the old man's pointers had been so accurate I'd begun to trust what he told me—that its switchback descent would take over an hour before I reached the stream. He'd cackled maniacally when he said it, I had no idea why.

I glanced down at my watch. It was still late morning. If there'd been a single touch of grace in my dawn debacle, it was this serendipitous gift of time.

Fifty or sixty yards down the trail, a rattlesnake slithered across the red dirt in front of me. Two or three more buzzed threateningly beneath shaded rocks or sagebrush as I crept nervously on. Eventually I could hear the river—began a harrowing, heart-throbbing creep through the waist-high switchgrass toward its bank. By the time I reached it, I'd seen or heard a half-dozen snakes more. My steps had become so slow, so measured, I felt like a man inching his way through a mine field. When I finally reached the water, my jaw was tight with anxiety and my clothes were soaked with sweat.

But what lay in front of me made my pulse throb even harder. Staring up the river, I saw a half-mile of open water an angler chances on only in his dreams. The stream wasn't wide, barely wider than the blacktop road I'd left two hours earlier, and only a few feet deep in its deepest runs. But every inch looked as if it would hold fish—a variety of riffles, pools, and undercut banks carved in the ratios God would create if he were an impassioned angler. And there was nothing to hinder a backcast but a few huge boulders. It was the first time in years of fly fishing that my hands literally trembled so visibly I had trouble stringing my rod.

I tied on a Pheasant-Tail Nymph. The first trout struck within seconds. So lofty by then were my expectations—the sight of the river building exponentially on the old man's hypnotic narrative—that I was a bit disappointed when the rainbow soon flopping in my net came to little more than three pounds. I caught another of the same size a couple of casts later, then a dozen more, the largest a six- or seven-pound brown, when a rise the shape of a manhole cover abruptly bulged the current twenty yards in front of me. Shaken, I stepped clumsily out of the river to change flies.

Transfixed by the still dissipating bulge, I'd dropped my flanks unthinkingly to rest on a flat rock when there sounded again that arid buzz nobody forgets who has ever heard it. Stumbling back into the water, I turned to glimpse the slitted eyes gleaming out from the snake's taut coils, mere inches from the shaded ledge where I was about to sit. It's a testament to the power of the place—the size of the rise I'd just witnessed—that the fear swelling in my stomach dulled my absorption only a minute or two before I steadied my hand and removed the fish-tattered nymph.

There was no sign of a hatch on the thigh-deep water, no further surface disturbance where the huge trout had risen. But I'd seen an abundance of grasshoppers in the switchgrass. Too benumbed or shaken to deliberate further, I plucked a Joe's Hopper from the box and greased it lightly. The fish still hadn't risen again—at least I hadn't seen it rise, my eyes flitting from the tippet to the menacing ledge behind me—but half a second after the big terrestrial slapped the water I was certain I was into the largest trout I'd ever hooked on a fly. My hands shook visibly again ten minutes later, when I landed and released it, a brown trout of such strength and mottled beauty a cry of pure joy leapt spontaneously from my throat.

I glanced again at my watch, blinked as the awareness registered that I'd been in the canyon for close to four hours. The fact astonished me.

For the first time since I reached the stream, I looked not at the water or the snake-infested shore. A glowing sun had dropped disturbingly close to the canyon's rim. I looked up at the trail—a serpentine red seam zigzagging up through the snake-infested rocks and sagebrush. The thought of walking out in the dark, even with the small flashlight that remained in my vest from my predawn hike that morning, was so harrowing I vowed I would fish only fifteen minutes longer, not a second more.

Seeing no more rises in the pool ahead of me, I made a quick, impulsive switch to the largest Matuka Streamer in my fly box. The sun had dropped low enough in the western sky that the dark water along the opposite bank flowed enticingly beneath an overhang of switch-grass, and though I had to quarter the fly upstream, dead-drifting it until the current's steady pull swept it under, I moved so quietly along the gravel bottom it seemed possible a trout might remain unspooked even directly across from me as I fished on.

I glanced once more at my watch a moment after the fish struck—saw that I would have to land it within eight minutes or break the most determined vow I had ever made. To that point I had little clue what was throbbing up through the line into my fingers. It was a good fish, a heavy fish, that I was sure of. A fish big or angry enough to lie sulking under the bank for as long as I yielded to its will.

But the fly was also big. And I'd switched to a 2X tippet when I tied it on, trusting that the shadowed water would make anything lighter unnecessary. There was also a final thought, if it can truly be said that a man *thinks* under such conditions: the fish seemed to be solidly hooked. It's always more feel than forensics in those first few moments after a strike, but the ticking watch had rendered any but the decision I quickly came to a moot point.

Hauling back harder on the rod than I had since my callow youth on a bass lake, I hit the sulking fish with a jolt that bent the rod almost double. The trout reacted at once, shooting out of the water in a detonation of flesh and spray. Crashing back into the water it held there for a single moment, as if fueling its fury into will, then did the gut-wrenching, intelligent thing an angler fears almost as much when fighting a large fish as the sight of his line tracking toward a tangle of roots or a fallen tree. It shot downstream, not upstream as I had prayed—bulled on into the choppy run below me with such strength and conviction I could only marvel at the reel's scream and the vanishing line. When my mind finally cleared I splashed stumbling down the river in the fish's wake—loosened the drag to let the brute run freer in the faint hope it might lose its sense of the hook's prick and slow enough I could recapture the lost line.

That it was by an order of magnitude the biggest trout I had ever been attached to was beyond question. A fish so large only a photo would confirm its length and girth. And the trout did in fact slow—even ended its violent run—held long enough in the current that I managed to reload nearly all of the depleted line. For the briefest of moments I felt the hope flare that it was all going to end with the fish, or some manageable part of him, wallowing in my net. And then the trout felt the alien hook once more—surged on downstream with a will that I knew, even as the next deathless seconds unfolded, was not going to let him slow again until he was free.

The snake struck when I slipped on a rock, plunging after the fish in the heavy current—shot my left hand blindly toward the shore trying not to fall. I felt the needle stabs in my wrist a millisecond before the tippet snapped and the fish was gone.

It was a large snake, as big around as my forearm. And a trout, a brown trout, that had been well and fairly hooked by my fly.

I hadn't been anywhere near the place for many years. But a few months ago, a trip west took me within fifty miles of it, and on an impulse I followed the county road that fed off the interstate toward the tiny hamlet where the ill-tempered old man had told the tale that cost me my left arm. The gas pumps were gone. All that remained was the cinder-block building, now a down-at-the-heels bar and café.

It was midafternoon. Late September. A plump, middle-aged woman behind the bar was the only person in there. Sliding onto a stool, I ordered a beer, and when she returned with it I told her why I'd stopped—told her I'd been there years earlier, in the heat of summer, and talked to an old codger whose name I never learned. I told her a little of what he'd told me, about a remote valley not far to the north that he'd called *the Devil's Arse*.

It was clear neither the old man nor the bizarre name meant anything to her.

I added that the place had a lot of rattlesnakes.

Her eyes lit with instant recognition. "Oh, you must mean Paradise Valley," she said. "It's real private. No one around here knows much about it at all. The word is it used to be crawlin' with snakes, back before it was bought by one of them Japanese corporations. They put in a herd of buffalo to graze it all down—built a fancy lodge and a helicopter pad that's right next to it, apparently. Now they fly in their top honchos and I suppose some of their clients for a few days of R and R. Or at least that's what folks say they do, I ain't never seen the place myself. Most of the year it just sets there idle, except for the staff, and none of them are from around here."

I finished the beer and thanked her for the information, rose to leave.

"Kind of a shame, ain't it?" she went on. "The waste, I mean—that it's used so little. I hear the fishin' up there's still purty good."

Fly

"Isn't that thing like hunting a tiger with a switch?"

"It sure feels like it today."

The river flowed down to the Oregon coast, the slate-dark pool just above its mouth ringed with spin fishermen. Their casting was so intent they appeared oblivious to the waves crashing onto the beach barely a stone's throw distant behind a thin, windswept spit of sand. The fly fisherman was from the Midwest. An alien. His short stabbing casts fell impotently among the dozens of lines that angled past and sometimes across each other from the opposite shorelines. Backlit by the evening sun, they glinted like a giant web spun out of monofilament. In such tight quarters, the nine-foot rod might as well have been a switch in his hand.

The edgy question was the first thing the grizzled man on his left had said to him in hours. His throat tightening with irritation, he cast the roe-colored fly a few inches farther, watched it slap the water less than twenty feet past his rod tip and slowly vanish into the pool.

"Fish on!"

Reflexively, he reeled in at the cry—let his envious gaze hold on the lucky fisherman across the river only after the tiny ball of yarn was safely back in his hand. More than once, in similar mob scenes on Lake Michigan, he'd seen what could happen in the absence of this unspoken protocol. *Combat fishing.* A clot of men casting in conditions all of them hated but were forced to tolerate because the salmon were in and every fisher within five hundred miles who gave a damn had gotten wind of it.

Inevitably, sooner or later, someone hooked up and twenty yards down the shoreline another fisherman, clueless or belligerent, ignored the courtesy and kept on casting—cast until the moment his hook snagged the planing line and both men were playing the same fish: the guy who had actually hooked it still unaware; the other honestly, or feigning, the same. Ten or twenty seconds would pass, maybe a minute, both rods still bent and throbbing. Then the fish was abruptly off and the lines went slack as the first angler reeled in cursing his luck and found the other guy's hook snared across his own.

He had once seen a man so incensed at the recognition, a construction worker from Milwaukee with a thick eastern European accent, he'd chased the offender a hundred yards up the shoreline brandishing his "priest"—a foot-long chunk of iron pipe used to administer the last rites to a landed salmon. The pursuit ended only when both fishermen were so winded they staggered to some gasping, curse-filled standoff in the dark.

The fly fisherman wanted none of that here. He'd grown up with conflict—it was a way of life in his part of the city—and it always made him nervous. Mercifully, since his awkward arrival at the crowded pool five hours earlier, things had stayed cool. The men beside and across from him all did as he had done, however grudgingly—reeled in and stood watching impatiently, saying little or nothing, until the hooked salmon was played out and the fist-pumping fisherman dragged it flopping onto the sand.

Still, despite the absence of any apparent rednecks, the conditions were such that every few minutes a pair of lines got snagged. No one else felt obliged to reel in then. Their own lines remained in the water until the next triumphant cry signaled that another fish was on.

Staring at the jubilant angler across the river, he changed the color of his fly once more—sent another short stabbing cast into the pool. How many times had he done it, reeled dutifully in and stood grimly watching yet another man's good fortune, in the hours since he'd walked the mile and a half down the tire-rutted beach and crossed to the ocean side of the stream? How many fish had he seen landed, or lost? Thirty? Fifty? However many it had been, he'd long since passed the point where fishing a fly felt less like commitment than some pig-headed farce.

No matter what color yarn he used, and he'd tried at least a dozen, a yarn fly in these conditions was simply not going to work. No fly in his vest would work. Even if the tippet were weighted with split shot, it wasn't going to sink deep enough—get down near the bottom where the fish lay—in the short drifts that were all his cramped space allowed. To lengthen them risked horning in on another man's jealously guarded slice of water. Pushing for a few extra feet, he'd already cast across the lines of both men flanking him, caused a pair of wordless but pointed entanglements. The "hunting a tiger with a switch" barb had come a few minutes after the last.

He stopped casting and took a more reflective look at the cluster of spin fishermen bordering the pool. Most of them wore camo or out-sized gray sweatshirts, hoods raised against the biting wind off the ocean. A few sat on buckets, their butts sagging over the anchovies they all seemed to be using as bait. But aside from these basic facts, he could make no easy generalizations. The men were of all ages. Body types. Even level of skill, within the narrow range that divided success from failure in this kind of bait fishing. The one thing he felt sure all of them had in common was the perception that he was a fool.

"Fish on!"

He reeled in once more as yet another cry broke across the river and the maddening scenario played out again. The fisherman jerked back on his thick-shafted rod. Set the hook deep. Hauled and bent and hauled again until the overmatched salmon rose wallowing to the surface, trying to shake the weighted rig in its jaw. After a few more seconds of weakening resistance, this fish too lay on the shoreline. "He's a fresh one—silver as hell!" the guy's buddy yelped, straddling it as he picked up a nearby chunk of driftwood. He clubbed the flopping salmon twice on the head, then a third time, before tossing aside the ready-to-hand priest.

The fly fisherman kept the tuft of yarn in his hand, his mind a snarl of conflicted emotions, as the guy who'd caught the heavy fish lugged it up to his Styrofoam cooler and dropped it on the sand. It could have been him, back on Sturgeon Bay a dozen years earlier. Hell, it *still* could be him, he told himself glumly. All he'd have to do was switch to bait.

Staring across the water at the dead fish, he considered it. Several anchovies lay awash in the frothy chop near his neoprenes, discarded by a fisherman who a couple of hours earlier had dumped his bucket, lit a celebratory cigar, and hauled his pair of salmon back across the stream to his ATV. The bait remained there for the taking. It would look weird, casting it with a fly rod, but he was far past the point where that made any difference to him. He knew the technique, both from his own bait-fishing days and from observing the crusty pair of older men beside him. Few things were simpler. Thread on a sinker. Tie on a hook and pierce it up through the skull of the baitfish. Toss the rig in the pool and wait for the light tap, tap, tap or the stronger jerk that signaled a salmon's deeper take. Then haul your ass back up the beach like you've anchored your dart in a whale and watch all the other bastards grimly reel their lines in as your own yelp of triumph touches the roof of the world.

He glanced down again at the foam-coated anchovies. Touched the upper pocket of his vest for the tube of split shot he carried there. A half dozen would be enough to sink his hook to the bottom, where the salmon lay. Why couldn't he do it? The desire to hook a fish burned in him like lust, like the crackling fire one of the spin fishermen had started on the beach behind him, and it was clear that the sun sinking behind it in the cloud-streaked sky would allow less than an hour more of fishing time, at best. In the intensity of his focus, he hadn't realized how many of the throng had already departed. At least forty vehicles—ATVs and 4X4 pickups—had sat parked on the beach when he'd arrived. Now fewer than half that remained.

He glanced again at the tight-lipped fisherman on his left, motionless except for a calloused forefinger moving with the sluggish current tugging at his line. Barely a dozen words had passed between them in the hours since he'd claimed his own wedge of shoreline—stepped quickly into the niche that had briefly opened there.

Impulsively, he broke the silence.

"Quite a few guys have left."

The older man turned his head and stared at him evenly, a thin smile seaming his wrinkled face. The thick finger still moved almost imperceptibly across his line.

"You're not from around here," he said.

The words were simply a statement of fact, carried neither interest nor apparent hostility.

"No," the fly fisherman responded. "Illinois."

"Mmmm."

Nothing more was said for several minutes. The spin fisherman reeled slowly in, tossed the mangled baitfish into the river, and stabbed the hook into the rubber handle of his rod.

"Let me give you a piece of advice," he said, reeling up the last slack inches of monofilament until it strummed faintly beneath his thumb. "I don't think you've noticed, but this is a tidal river. You're going to be stuck out here all night if you don't cross it pretty damn soon."

The fly fisherman wasn't stupid. Was even a little vain about the depth of his experience—the skills that through the past decade he'd learned outdoors. Yet the words struck him like a fist in the gut. How could he have been so blind? So focused on catching a salmon it hadn't even faintly registered that while a sizable knot of fishermen still stood fifty yards across the pool from him, only three—the grizzled stranger and his two buddies by the fire—remained on his side of the stream.

He knew it was a tidal river. But glancing anxiously downstream, he felt another clutch in his stomach at the recognition that the shallows he'd splashed across on his arrival were now at least waist-deep, possibly more. In all the time he had stood there, fruitlessly casting, lulled by the hypnotic roar of the breakers slamming the beach, it hadn't once occurred to him that he could be trapped.

The clutch in his gut wasn't fear. He knew there wasn't any danger, as long as he remained on the side where he stood. But the prospect of remaining there all night, chilled to the bone and sleepless, stirred an emotion that at that moment felt stronger than fear. He knew it was bred of jealousy—frustration—the sight of all those thrashing fish dragged by men with lesser true angling skills up onto the sand. He also knew why he'd unconsciously tuned out the river's slow, unceasing rise.

A few feet from the fire behind him, where the crusty old guy now stood drinking with his buddies, their large, mud-spattered pickup sat parked on the sand. Somehow the fact hadn't registered that its bed was enclosed by a camper. The three men were obviously going to stay through the night, drinking beer and grilling steaks or salmon, then sleep five or six hours before rising to fish again sometime after dawn. All that had escaped him. Maybe only somebody from his landlocked part of America would have ignored the fact that such a vehicle could have been driven there only at low tide. Or did his real blindness lie elsewhere, in some deeper repression? A refusal to accept the fact it could be driven there at all.

That there were men who would steer a truck across a tidal river in the face of ocean breakers lashing the beach fifty yards away, you couldn't live in America today without knowing it—swallowing the fact that motorized vehicles could reach all but the most isolated places, and that there were plenty of gearheads who lived to drive them even there. But that reality had never been easy for him to accept, and it was harder now. Growing up in the city, he hadn't discovered the true outdoors until his early twenties, when he spent a month bumming through the Upper Peninsula of Michigan living on beans and panfish and sleeping in a cheap tent. The peace and solitude he'd found there had left a lasting mark.

He stared again at the trio of aging men behind him. In the chill October evening, they hunched warming themselves by their campfire, toeing chunks of driftwood with their heavy boots and clutching the cans of beer in their weathered hands. The bitter irony didn't escape him. Now that their departure had finally left him room to cast a fly, the rising tide had forced him to stop fishing unless he forded the river—crossed back over to the other side of the pool where he'd find himself wedged in once more.

The prospect was just barely more appealing than quitting altogether. His thoughts held on that option—the hours immediately in front of him: The long walk back up the beach to his rental car. A solitary meal and sterile motel room. Then the remaining drive up the coast to the airport for his flight back to O'Hare. That would be the end of it, after three strikeless days flogging the upper Rogue and this smaller river, which he'd come to only when he could no longer deny the fact that several weeks without rain had left his favorite streams nearly barren of fish. There were salmon here. But it was the last place he'd ever have chosen to be.

Distracted, he lifted the rod and cast again—felt so unburdened by the extra feet of line flowing out behind him he overshot his target and knew before the rod bent on the hurried retrieve that he'd once again fouled another man's line. The owlish fisherman glared across the pool at him, spat disgustedly into the water as he reeled the tangled lines in.

He looked helplessly away as the stranger labored to untangle the snarled hooks. Up and down the shoreline, the couple of dozen other men who remained all seemed to be staring back at him. Two or three were smiling, maybe even indulgently. The faces of the rest had the look a Wall Street banker might have seen driving his new Ferrari past a crowded bus stop in Detroit.

The look stung him—the perception that he was an *elitist*. He, Frank Konczyk, who'd grown up in south Chicago and come to fly fishing not out of some birthright or sense of privilege but simply because the first time he'd ever hooked a fish on a fly rod he'd realized—known instantly—that the sport was to bait fishing what a porterhouse steak was to a Big Mac. The loaned rod had been a friendly stranger's. The impulse to pick it up and try it, a total lark. And the fish he had somehow managed to hook, a scrappy ten-inch smallmouth.

It had been enough. Within a year he was squirreling away whatever money he could spare for what eventually became this annual autumn trip to the Pacific coast.

If that made him an elitist, so be it. He didn't look down on any of them—their spinning gear or their use of bait or their styrofoam coolers. At that moment, he probably craved a salmon at the end of his line more than any of them did.

Some of it was ego, he'd admit that—the wish that he could *show* them the native steelhead he'd caught and released a year earlier on the Umpqua. The skill it took to quarter the fly twenty yards across the river into a knifing wind under a cedar's overhanging bough.

So, okay. *Ego.* But beneath it, something more than ego, something like the mixed feelings he guessed must lie behind the so-called calling of a religious zealot—the compulsion both to sing it out to the masses yet keep it as secret as a bed of morel mushrooms you've chanced on deep in the woods. Done well, fly fishing gave him the same quiet pleasure—but a lot higher high—that he got using first-rate tools on a precision project, where the tolerances were close to zero and the slightest mistake meant the whole job went up in smoke. That, maybe even more than the solitude and the natural beauty of the settings, was what had captured him in the sport.

He stared again across the river, where the rankled fisherman was still working to free the lines his miscast fly had fouled. Unable to do anything but stand there watching, he let his mind wander on.

Why did it mean so much to him, catching a fish? No, catching one wasn't it exactly. It was more the *playing* of the fish that mattered, though the phrase had always struck him as absurd. *Playing* was the last word he'd ever use to explain how it felt.

It wasn't that he was indifferent to the catching. Far from it. He loved to tail or beach a good fish, and though he released most of them, the ones he kept to cook and eat were a separate, quieter pleasure—like a good dessert after that porterhouse steak on a night when he hadn't eaten all day just to heighten the taste. But no, that comparison wasn't quite right either, and a cliché to boot. It was more like enjoying the building of the hand more than the actual winning of the pot when you were playing poker. Maybe the only sense in which the word *play* fit at all.

The train of thought had led the angler beyond anyplace his mind felt comfortable, and he mumbled to himself self-consciously, *"Goddamn, man, get a grip."* He stared again across the river—felt a wash of gratitude as the spin fisherman finally freed his fly.

The bottom line was that he knew him—had *been* him. However weird his tastes might appear to them now, he'd been *all* these hooded men with their camo coveralls and tackle boxes full of hooks and sinkers and their heavy, sloshing buckets of bait. Things changed, and you rolled with it. You never knew when or where a spark might turn to flame. Catching a fish on a bit of yarn, or getting dragged against your will to an opera—discovering against all odds that you actually enjoyed it. That much of the mystery of life, at least, he had learned.

The thought lifted his spirits. He might not be able to catch a fish when every other sonofabitch on the coast was catching one, but he was standing by a salmon river with a fly rod in his hand. It might not be as good as it got, but damned close.

Then something happened the angler had never seen before, a scene that left him transfixed. The burly spin fisherman whose line he'd tangled had rebaited his hook—cast it in a high looping arc toward the middle of the river. But before the weighted anchovy could sink below the surface a hovering gull dove and snatched it away. The bird managed to strip out forty or fifty feet of line before the startled fisherman regained his bearings and flipped the reel bail—stopped it abruptly in midair. For at least a minute the gull struggled against the retrieve, its wings beating the air as it was dragged yawing like a broken kite toward the earth. Strained to the breaking point, the taut monofilament sawed back and forth across the sky, until at last the bird lay grounded under the rod tip. Pinning a flapping wing with his boot, the now even more aggravated fisherman grabbed the line and severed it with a quick thrust of his buck knife. The freed bird flew away with the hook still buried in its craw.

Stunned, the fly fisherman knew with the force of revelation what he must do. Turning on his heel, he walked upstream along the beach, away from the crowd—his eyes fixed on a distant bend where the river disappeared into a stand of pine trees. For the first time in hours he felt liberated. Light-footed. Free of self-consciousness or doubt. Behind him he heard one of the aging men by the campfire mutter under his breath "What the hell's that dumb cluck up to now?" Then, louder, to his back, *"No way you're gonna get across up there!"* He raised an arm slightly to acknowledge the warning but didn't turn as he walked on. He'd belatedly remembered the book of matches sealed in his inside vest pocket, but they wouldn't have mattered. He'd have poached a place next to their fire if it had come to that.

The matches would make that humiliation unnecessary. There was so much driftwood littering the beach he could easily build his own fire—sleep on the sand and rise at daybreak. Fish for a good three more hours and still have enough time, if he drove nonstop, to make his flight home. He didn't have a tide table, but however high the water was, he'd get across it. Would strip naked and swim if he had to, carrying his rod and pants over his head.

If all that made him crazy, he could live with it. You probably had to be a little nuts just to care so much about catching a fish. Especially laboring to catch one on a few shreds of synthetic wool.

The yarn fly. From the beginning, despite or maybe because of the fact he'd been publicly embarrassed learning how to create one, it had been his fly of choice. An old couple in a mom-and-pop tackle shop on the Skagit had tried to teach him how to tie it. Both of them were probably gone now, as their ramshackle little store no doubt was too. But the angler vividly remembered the old man's gnarled yet still nimble fingers moving over the strand of leader—his reverse loops over the hook shank and the sudden, wondrous moment when the snell cinched down on its perfect tight coils behind the eye. His own bumbling efforts to duplicate the process were no less vivid—the repeated attempts when he came close but just . . . could not . . . quite *get it.*

Shamed, he'd thanked the couple profusely for their patient instruction as he hurried out of the store. They'd clearly been unaware that he'd stopped outside the door to retie a shoelace, overheard their postmortem exchange.

"You think he'll ever get it?"

"That fella? Not much of a chance. He might know a bunch o' things where he comes from, back in the city, but he don't seem to have a clue out here."

Reaching the bend, the angler stopped, looked down at the tiny ball of chartreuse fluff in his hand. The fact that a fish as magnificent as a salmon or steelhead could be caught on such a bit of nothing had never lost its hold on him. Hemingway as usual had said it best, in words that stuck the moment he'd first read them: *To bring such a fish in was something worth waiting many days for.* He'd add only that the fish should be taken on a fly.

Staring across the water, he saw that the river was narrower, elbowed to the left—a good lie for a holding or cruising salmon, especially at dusk. Reachable with a good cast, yet shallow enough a single split shot would trail the fly down near the bottom, past a salmon's nose. Briefly he cursed himself for not fleeing the crowd at the river's mouth hours earlier—for hanging there more out of his chronic stubbornness than the obvious fact the pool was filled with fish.

It was different here. Different in every way, starting with a fact just as obvious. The absence of any other fisher at a bend on a fertile river was usually a sign no fish swam anywhere near. The recognition momentarily sobered him. Viewed from above, where the gods perched, a man casting shreds of wool into barren water was probably as fair an image as any of the absurd.

The fisherman didn't linger on such weighty thoughts now. His mind had returned to that place familiar to zealots, however crazy they might appear to the world at large. Mountain climbers. Cliff divers. The men who lived to amass billion-dollar fortunes and the smaller number who gave up everything to cloister themselves in some monastic cell. Like most of them, at least so he assumed, he was single. Childless. Probably in the eyes of a shrink, certifiably unhinged. He laughed softly at the thought—imagined his own eyes as they'd look at that moment, even to the other diehard fishermen whose web of lines he'd fled. The burning gaze of Picasso. Or a lot more likely, Charley Manson. Both of them were before his time—he'd seen only the indelible photographs. But it was the way his eyes felt to him as he scanned the pool for any sign of a fish.

He stood there, staring into the water, long enough that his body began to stiffen for lack of movement and the eyes began to glaze. But when the sign did in fact come he reacted instinctively. A single wake, unmistakable as a heartbeat, ruffled the glassy surface twenty yards in front of him—a furrow behind a blunt, swift-moving plow. His hands trembling, the fisherman lifted the rod and stripped out line, felt his lungs fill and his shoulders loosen as the nearly weightless fly shot across the river. It dropped a few inches from where he'd aimed it, three feet past the still furrowing vee.

His spirit soared higher. He'd been there before and the thrill never lessened, his chest pounding with anticipation. *A strike, and a solid hookup if he is lucky. The great silver fish leaping out of the river as the line flows on like spun silk through his hand . . .*

The FÜLODOG

My name's Cooper. I mention that at the outset because I'm the only one of our foursome without a nickname, unless "Coop" qualifies as such. The way we met is one of those bizarre scenarios that happen in life about as often as winning the lottery. For the four of us were—remain—as outwardly unmatched and ill suited to compatibility as any four American males of approximately the same middle age could be. Flash is a jeweler. Crawler cleans septic tanks. Martini's a tenured professor of classics at the local U. And me? Just say I'm a guy whose work résumé has enough listings it requires extra postage to mail.

And yet there we were, a potluck foursome of total strangers, teeing it up together at our local muni on the most glorious April morning any of us could recall.

It was the kind of day when you wake up after an endless winter and know at once you have to *do* something—have to *get out*. If we'd done the first thing that stirred in our blood—the thing each of us, unbeknownst to each other, wanted desperately to do—we'd have gone trout fishing. But that common bond was one of the last things we discovered about each other. Which is some kind of warped cosmic irony, for that glorious Saturday happened to be the opener of the trout season, and much as we longed to be out, we'd all privately sworn years earlier never again to join the stream-clogging hordes on opening day.

As a result, each of us arrived alone at the mangy little municipal course, toting our ill-matched, even mangier sets of golf clubs. None of us had ever played more than a couple of times a year. The starter rolled his eyes and put us together, no doubt in the faint hope of consolidating the damage to the fairways and greens. None of us took the game seriously. Maybe because of this near-equal ineptitude, we agreed after the round to play again a few days later, and have hacked our way around the course together a couple of times a month ever since.

But fishing for trout is a different story. Though, as I mentioned, it wasn't until our third or fourth round together that this mutual passion came to light. As I recall, it happened on the fifteenth tee when Crawler hit one of his skulled hooks and Flash barked something across the fairway about "another worm killer." To which Crawler drawled in response "Damn straight, I'll use 'em out on Crooked Creek tomorrow afternoon."

From that point on, in that post-match hour when most golfers sit in the clubhouse bar rehashing their rounds, the four of us invariably hunched over our drinks arguing about trout fishing. And it was in those heated exchanges—a kind of culmination of them, I suppose it's fair to say—that the FÜLODOG contest was born.

From the beginning, the heart of our endless squabbling was the question of how best to fish for trout. "Best" as in most effective, most enjoyable, most efficient, most *etc., etc.* You name it, we argued over it, with about as much chance of resolution as there is that any of us will ever break a 100 on the links. Flash fishes spinners. Crawler is a garden hackle purist. And Martini's nickname is Martini because his loyalty to dry flies exceeds even that to his post-round libation, which he unfailingly tells the clubhouse barman to mix with "just a baby's breath of vermouth." Me? I guess you could say I'm eclectic. I'll switch, even bait and switch, until I hit upon something that works.

When that's your modus operandi, it's hard to be as preferential about any single method of catching a trout as my three hacker compadres. Which is why I've never said much when the arguments get heated, and why they finally coerced me into submission to be the contest judge. They had to pick up my bar tab half a dozen times before I finally agreed to do it. But finally, worn down, I gave in. The three of them set the terms. The winner of the contest would get a filet dinner at the best restaurant in town, courtesy of the other two. My tab would be picked up by all of them, as long as I didn't order anything spendier than a hamburger steak.

As I recall, after these basic ground rules had been sorted out, the conversation that followed went something like this.

Crawler: So what're we gonna call it?

Me: Call what?

Crawler: This award I'm gonna win.

Martini had a twinkle in his eye that I alone seem to have noticed. Smiling drolly, he responded, "You have zero chance of winning it. But if you want a name, let's just dub it the Lord of the Anglers award."

Crawler shot him a long glare beneath the brim of his dirty Cubs cap. "I don't like *Angler*," he croaked. "I've never *angled* in my goddamned life. Makes you sound like some frickin' wuss."

"All right then," Martini countered, smiling thinly. "How about the *Fishing* Lord?"

He took another sip of his drink and set the glass down authoritatively, the olive bouncing like a plump green dancer in the stream-clear gin. Crawler stared at him dubiously. Flash snorted. I stifled a laugh too at the title's pretentiousness—assumed the two of them were thinking the same thing.

I should have known better.

Flash: I don't know. It seems a little, I dunno . . . a little *blah* to me. I mean, it doesn't even say I'll be the lord of fishing for *trout*.

Martini: What's at the top of any sane man's aquatic hierarchy? The trout. That's clear by definition. Adding anything to "Fishing Lord," ipso facto, is redundant.

Crawler jabbed me with his elbow and raised his eyebrows in "What'd he just say?" incomprehension. Before I could help him the other two rolled on.

Flash: I still say it's too . . . too *generic*.

He took a hard gulp of his own habitual post-round drink, a Pink Squirrel, his gold tooth glinting in the light. Martini shook his head, then gave a pitying, indulgent sigh. Plucking the olive slowly from his empty glass, he signaled the bartender for his check and surrendered. "I suppose we could call it the Fishing Über Lord," he said.

Nobody responded. Crawler poked me in the ribs again.

"I think it means something like 'everything,'" I mumbled to him. "Lord of the Angling Universe."

Nobody said anything more for some time. The three of them just sat staring at each other. Finally Crawler spoke.

"I kind of like it," he said. "Classes it up."

Martini rolled his eyes and was reaching for his wallet when I stopped him. "Before you leave," I said, "if I'm going to judge this thing, I need to get something straight." The way they'd set the contest up, they would all call in sick (or as Martini insisted on calling it, "take a personal day") the following Wednesday, and would fish in separate, two-hour slots on a prime quarter-mile stretch of Crooked Creek. I was sure there would be a raging argument over the preferred time slot, but in fact there was none at all. Flash, the spinner fisherman, wanted the two hours just after dawn, when shadows covered the water. Martini wanted to fish his dries late in the morning, when the hatches were most likely to come on. That left the two hours in between for Crawler, who had so much faith in the night crawlers that were his favorite bait he said he didn't "give a shit" what time of day or night he fished them. I would trail behind each fisherman during his two-hour stint, recording the catch in a notebook, then join them all in the clubhouse bar with my verdict. We'd then meet again that night for the payoff, the Fishing Über Lord award—the FÜL—at the restaurant.

The three of them remained at the table, impatient, waiting for me to go on.

"You've told me where to be, at what time of the day," I said, "even how many feet I'm supposed to walk or stand behind you." They all nodded smugly, their faces registering supreme confidence that neither of the others had a snowball's chance in hell of winning the award. "What you haven't told me is exactly *what* I'm supposed to judge."

"Whaddaya mean?" Crawler blurted. "You're choosin' the best fisher-man. Namely me," he added grinning. "Simple as that. What the hell else is there to know?"

"Just one thing," I said, grinning back at him. "What do you mean by *best*?"

He stared at me as if I had the IQ of a gerbil. "The best *fisherman!*" he growled. "How hard is that to figure out?"

I paused long enough to let each of my next few words sink in.

"*Best* as in *biggest* fish caught? *Most* fish? *First* fish after the clock starts ticking? Or *best* as in different *kinds* of trout taken? Crooked has all three—brown, brook, and rainbow. Or do you mean the guy who *casts* the best, or *lands* a trout the most skillfully, or wa—"

"Okay, okay, we get the picture," Flash cut me off. "I guess you're right. We need to be a little more specific."

It's probably simplest to say about the next hour that three more rounds of drinks were consumed, the decibel level got higher and higher, and the three of them finally arrived at what was less a collective decision than a half-snockered, grudging capitulation. The Fishing Über Lord would be whoever I named him to be. None of them was happy about it. Even Martini had gotten so exercised, arguing for the *number* of trout taken, that he'd shed his elbow-patched cardigan and slammed it down on his chair. But it had eventually become clear, even to the three of them, that they could sit there debating the point until Doomsday without reaching an agreement. Exhausted by the drink and the effort, they'd slumped back into silence when Crawler said one thing more.

"Damned hard to have much confidence when you don't know what the hell somebody's lookin' for," he muttered, glaring at me. "It's like tryin' to guess the strike zone of a blind ump."

"You don't have a strike zone," Martini sniffed. "Trout sucking down a worm don't strike."

Crawler peeled the wrappers off three sticks of Juicy Fruit and popped the gum into his mouth.

"I could say somethin' about fly fisherwomen," he croaked, "but I don't wanna insult your gender. Alls I'll say is this. If these are the rules, we can't call it the . . . whatever the hell that *Ü* means. . . . We can't call it the FÜL award."

In light of how much he'd taken to the name earlier, this surprised all of us. Finally Flash said, "Okay, I'll bite. Why not?"

"'Cause we all know who the real lord is," he fired back. "I said I was in, and I'm not gonna bail on you, no matter how this doofus is gonna judge it." He shot another bleary glance in my direction. "But we've gotta add something. Whoever wins, it's only gonna be for *that one day*."

"One day," Martini repeated.

"Damned right," growled Crawler.

"The FÜL(ODO)," Flash said, certifying it, his gold tooth flashing. "The Fishing Über Lord (One Day Only)."

Though they'd had to bribe me to judge it, I was privately looking forward to Wednesday morning, primed with curiosity at how the thing would play out. For despite the countless clubhouse hours we'd spent talking about trout fishing, the bald fact was that I'd never actually *seen* any of them fish—didn't have a verifiable clue whether their self-testaments to their prowess fell within the permissible limits of bibulous exaggeration or were simply hot air. The curiosity pricked me out of bed and on to Crooked Creek a good half-hour before my scheduled meeting with Flash, who rolled up in his red Corvette a few minutes later. His spinning rod was loaded and ready at the crack of dawn, dangling a little silver and gold Mepps.

I guess maybe the best way to describe the two hours that followed is to say that he put a reverse Charles Barkley on me. That is, it was one of those times when you see something that runs so counter to your expectations you don't know whether to laugh or cry. In Barkley's case it's watching a world-class athlete—a huge guy so graceful and nimble on the basketball court he could leave you gasping—try to hit a golf ball with a swing that Whistler's mother would have been ashamed to display.

Flash's case was exactly the reverse. A guy so inept on the golf course the term "hacker" was a compliment, who from the first deft flick of his wrist with that lightweight little Shakespeare had the finesse of a Matisse wielding a brush. In those early morning shadows, I trailed him up the grassy shoreline as he knelt, stretched, hunkered, and hovered, all the time darting that tiny Mepps into places no other fisherman I'd ever seen would have dared to try. Undercut banks. Overhanging branches. Six-inch throats of current between encroaching beds of watercress. In that first hour he caught and released a dozen trout, the largest a seventeen-inch rainbow. He didn't do quite as well in the second hour, when the sun reached the water, but still brought another five to his net.

When his time was up we sat back on the bridge near our cars, munching the cinnamon rolls and sipping from the thermos of cappuccino he'd picked up at Starbucks on his way out. I wasn't sure whether they qualified as a bribe. Neither of us said anything for some time.

"Good job," I finally said noncommittally, taking the last roll.

He stood up and brushed the crumbs off his fleece vest.

"Should have landed that big brown I lost in those willow roots," he murmured. "That was a hell of a big fish."

A half-hour later, several minutes after his chosen starting time, Crawler's battered 4X4 crawled slowly down the hill. You could never mistake the old septic cleaner's vehicle, with its painted logo "Your Bathroom Ain't a Poker Table. A Flush Beats a Full House." He rolled to a rattling stop and climbed out, clutching an Ugly Stik and a ratty knapsack stuffed so full it looked about to burst at the seams. After he'd pulled a pair of folding aluminum lawn chairs from the creaking rear end of the pickup, we set off downstream. A hundred yards below the bridge a massive logjam, the aftermath of a flash flood the previous summer, had created a deep, swirling pool so full of snags and underbrush even Flash had made only a couple of cautious casts into it two hours before. Wheezing under his load, Crawler plopped the chairs down and rigged up. Two minutes later, a gob of red wigglers that looked like a baby octopus plopped into the water behind a chain of split shots that resembled a steel rosary.

He'd turned his back to me when he tied on his hook, so I wasn't sure what type or size that gaggle of worms was clinging to. "Want a brew?" he croaked, turning back to me and popping open a Budweiser. I declined, and for the next ten minutes we sat there simply killing time as he lounged back sipping the beer. Then I watched wide-eyed as the rod tip began to dance, he slowly lifted it from its holder, and hit the fish so hard the biggest trout I'd seen in at least five years soon lay flopping on the gravel shore. However much one might disdain bait-dunkers, the way Crawler had threaded the big brown out through the tangled maze of submerged branches was a hell of an impressive feat—even more impressive when he again turned his back secretively so I couldn't see exactly what he was doing, and released the fish.

"I thought you kept them," I blurted.

He watched the huge trout sink slowly back into the depths, then shambled back up the bank and picked up his beer.

"Not all of 'em, ya dumb shit," he muttered, grinning. "The big 'uns ain't worth crap in the fryin' pan." He glanced down at his watch. "Anyways, I still got plenty o' time."

I'll say this about Crawler, he was as good as his word. By the time he'd sent me out into the woods for some branches and kindling, he'd caught six more fish, the smallest pair—a couple of thirteen-inchers—fat browns that he quickly gutted and skinned and dropped into a plastic bag filled with cornmeal. By the time the shoreline fire had died down into a glowing bed of coals, he'd caught and released three more, the last one close to twenty inches long.

"I'd say that's 'bout enough for today," he mumbled, releasing it and wiping his hands on his jeans. "I could eat the ass end of a skunk."

Sliding his chair up to the fire, he popped open another Bud and dropped the two cleaned fish into an iron skillet sizzling with bacon grease. Then he reached into the seemingly bottomless knapsack and pulled out a logger-sized helping of onions and sliced spuds. I spent the last half-hour of his allotted fishing time scarfing down the best stream-side lunch I'd ever eaten. And it was still the near side of eleven o'clock in the morning. Maybe the meal tasted so good because I finally took him up on that beer.

"I don't know if you'll tell me this," I said, as he doused the fire and picked up his gear for the short walk back to the bridge. "But the curiosity's killing me. You never lost a rig, let alone a fish, in that logjam. How the hell did you do it? I mean, I know about the string of shot, that's an old steelheader's trick. But you never even *hooked* a snag. That defies common sense."

His big bent-nosed face eyed me dubiously for so long I was sure he was going to shake his head and walk away. But instead it filled with a proud, crooked-tooth grin.

"Check this out," he said simply, plucking the rig he'd used from the dinged metal box in his jeans pocket. I stared at it, still not sure what I was staring at. I don't know much about bass fishing, but I'm almost positive what he'd done was take one of those weedless large-mouth lures and modified it for trout.

Crawler's pickup had barely crawled up the hill and out of sight when Martini's Prius rolled crisply from the other direction down to the bridge. "Damn," I muttered to myself, stretched out on the grass beside my car. My belly was so full all I wanted at that point was a long nap in the warming sun, and I groaned at his prompt arrival. But I'd signed on for all three of them—knew the next two hours were now the classics professor's, not my own.

Martini was as meticulous in his angling preparations as he was lining up a putt, which is to say he took forever. As I implied earlier, when fish aren't hitting I'll try just about anything short of a stick of dynamite to catch a trout, though, the amazing feats I'd witnessed earlier that morning notwithstanding, I think almost any sane person has to be a fool not to prefer taking them on a fly. Still, I was unprepared for Martini's thoroughness when we finally stopped walking upstream. He took the water temperature; turned over rocks and analyzed the microscopic life forms he found there through a magnifying glass; stomach-pumped the first small brookie he caught before releasing it, then peered even more intently at the tiny dollop of goop he'd sucked out.

I actually dozed off watching him, lying on a grassy slope—was still barely sentient as he changed flies and crept a few quiet steps farther upstream. He'd chosen a long, flat stretch of water Crawler probably wouldn't have considered if the other option was a sewage treatment plant. And I'd seen enough of Flash's preferences to know he would have given the pool, at most, two or three desultory flicks of the wrist as he hastened past.

Martini was different. And I mean that in every possible sense of the word. I'm just skilled enough as a fly fisherman to be fairly sure he used three different types and sizes in the next hour—a small dun, which I think was a Blue Wing Olive; an even smaller fly, possibly a trico; and then a midge so nondescript and tiny it could have rested comfortably on an ant's rear end. He caught fish on all of them, especially the last one—so many fish I lost count after twenty-five. None were large—the biggest a fat, fourteen-inch brookie—but if the words "putting on a clinic" ever fit a trout fisher, what Martini did over those couple of hours has to qualify. And it wasn't just the number of fish he caught. His casts were as economical, yet as elegant and free-flowing, as his golf swing was quick and cramped.

Only two or three sporadic dimples still broke the surface of the placid pool when he stepped out and strode back down the shore-line. A few feet past me he stopped to lift something out of a bed of watercress—a chilled bottle of Chablis. I'd apparently been so drowsy I hadn't noticed earlier when he took it from the rear pocket of his vest. Back at the bridge, he produced from the Prius's trunk a wicker basket containing a baguette and a wedge of Brie. I don't know what he was thinking as we sat quietly on the bridge munching and sipping the terrific wine. But I sure as hell know what I was thinking—how damned *hard* it was going to be to name one of these fishermen the best, even for a single day. I'd long since dismissed their bribes, if that's what they were, as part of the final equation, even though I'd stuffed myself like a pig on all three. But how could I rank the feats I'd witnessed over the past few hours? It was apples and oranges—or more accurately, pot roast and duck a l'orange. I'd have had an easier time trying to choose the most beautiful body on a Mediterranean nude beach.

No doubt a bad analogy, when one of the trio was Crawler. But the guy had arguably shown me the most innovative angling technique I'd seen. Who was I to say it didn't qualify because he did it with a gob of worms? Flash had clearly been, well, the *flashiest*. And Martini had taken me to places Lee Wulff would have been impressed by.

It obviously was going to be impossible to name one of them. But what the hell, I shrugged, pulling back into town after racking my brain for over an hour. I was the judge. It might not be as good as being the king, but at least it meant a free meal.

I picked up my cell phone at that point and sent a text message to all three of them. I told them I was too stuffed to join them at the club-house or eat at the appointed hour, thanks to their generous offerings, and was going to change our dinner reservation from seven to nine. Then I shut the phone off, knowing each of them would be back at me within seconds, wanting to know who had won. The last thing I did before driving on home and taking a long nap was stop at the local Cabela's and spend twenty bucks on a few items I'd decided I would need.

All three of them were sitting at a corner table when I walked into the steakhouse at the revised hour. It was clear that even Martini, nursing his favorite drink, was edgy—waiting for the verdict I had pledged to give. Crawler's Bud looked like a bludgeon in his beefy, white-knuckled fingers. Before things got any tenser, I made another impulsive decision and sat down.

"Gentlemen," I croaked, tugging at my shirt collar, "before we move on to the formalities, let's enjoy our dinner. The filets are on me."

I dropped my tote bag on the floor and signaled to the waiter. The three of them looked at each other, then back at me, stunned. For any of us to voluntarily pick up a tab was as likely as stringing together a run of birdies. Suspicion was written all over their dubious faces, but I hoped the gesture might placate them a little when I finally announced the decision I'd made.

And so we ate, sipped our post-dessert brandies—even puffed on the cigars Flash had brought to pass around after he'd won. Getting him to do it *beforehand* took some doing. None of them was happy, in fact, when I kept insisting that no award worthy of the name was ever given before the celebratory dinner was done. Besides, wasn't I the judge? In the end they all went along, grudgingly. I was just trying to delay things to the last possible moment, then turn tail and get the hell out of Dodge.

"Boys," I finally said, clearing my throat and standing. "I know you're all on pins and needles, waiting for me to name the winner of this . . . this truly illustrious award. Though it's been in existence for only five days, it's already clear that the . . . the FÜL(ODO) has become a prize of enviable merit. No decision I've ever been asked to make has been nearl—"

"Just tell us who won the fuckin' thing," Crawler grunted, cutting me off. "I gotta be on the tank tomorrow morning at dawn."

"Second," Flash barked, glancing at Martini, who nodded emphatically too.

The moment of truth had arrived. Clearing my throat once more, I picked the bag off the floor and extracted what I'd bought earlier—a carved, brightly painted replica of a brook trout, with three hooks I'd attached dangling from its wooden lip. One was a dry fly. The second a Mepps Spinner. The third a plastic worm.

"Here's the deal," I said, staring back at them. "You guys made me the judge and there's no court of appeal. But you have a choice. This can either be a traveling trophy—you each get it for four months—or the winner gets determined scientifically—objectively—through strict mathematical data. In that case, I'm in too. We play a round of golf for it, winner take all."

It's probably best not to describe the next hour, before they closed the restaurant on us and we were left to stand arguing out in the street. Suffice it to say that the round of golf was eventually played. I shot a 122, and won by six strokes. The single consolation for the three losers was that I finally yielded to their insistence that the word "Golf" be added to the award title. But I took the liberty of dropping the parentheses, which would have made my victory feel, let's be honest, a little *parenthetical*. The trophy, which now rests on my mantelpiece, is simply inscribed the FÜLODOG.

Last Cast

He had worn the vest for almost fifty years. Half a century. Worn it so often and so long only a few crinkled tangles remained on the wool patch and the once-tawny cloth had darkened with fly floatant and sweat. He held it briefly in his gnarled hands before shrugging it on over his shoulders, the satisfying weight of his fly boxes pulling the pockets down against his withered waist.

Unzipping them, he discarded all but the lightest box—a silver cache of a dozen tarnished squares holding the few nymphs and the self-tied dries that had served him best and longest: four or five Adamses, some Quill Gordons, a handful of Elk Hair Caddis whose peacock herl and bright red banding shone dimly in the room's predawn light. The remaining compartments held tinier flies—gray and black midges and Blue Wing Olives and assorted others so small a half dozen could have rested on the yellowed nail of his thumb. He dropped them all back into their accustomed slots but an unmatched pair, nondescript and nameless. Flies he'd bought ten or fifteen or thirty years earlier on the South Platte or the Madison or the Beaverkill. Or perhaps they too were flies he'd tied himself, working from a Swisher or a Schwiebert volume open on the table in front of him—flies he'd used once or twice or maybe never on the Kickapoo or Trout Run.

For years, against the advance of age, he had thought one of them would be the stream he would walk last. More than likely on a day whose finality he would recognize only later, looking wistfully back from some hospital bed or hospice, if by then he was still able to recognize anything at all. A room where, if the gods were benevolent, he'd recline comfortably after a stroke or broken hip.

Cancer was something else entirely.

He had switched off the lamp and reached the door when a last image rose and held briefly in the flood of memory. The first Minnesota trout he'd ever caught had come on a streamer, the only fly he'd felt confident fishing back then. Returning to the table, he opened one of the discarded boxes and removed three big Maribou Muddlers—by far the largest flies remaining in his collection. Unused for . . . how long? A decade? More? He had long since convinced himself that he no longer fished them because he'd come to prefer the delicacy of nymphs and dries—the pulse of a trout working up through a thin nine-foot leader. And he knew that this was true. But so too was the blunt fact that a streamer as he aged had become more difficult to fish, especially on big water, where wind and the sometime need to weight it could leave his arm heavy with labor and his brain fraught with the nervous thought of a hook in the neck or the eye. Yet now, staring down at the outsized flies in his hands, he realized with a sudden pang that he'd missed them. Missed that dramatic moment when the bellying line went taut across the surface of the water and the sudden throb of a heavy fish shot like electric current up through the tightened muscles of his arm.

The grim irony of his situation hadn't escaped him. His was the kind of diagnosis so dire that one's closest friends and family, if you had either and lived almost anywhere else in the country, would have reflexively responded with urgent pleas to see a specialist at the Mayo Clinic. "Damn the expense, the travel. Get a second opinion. They're the best in the world." But when one lived in Rochester, and Mayo had given both the shocking first and the dreaded second diagnoses—the last from a world-renowned oncologist—there was no court of appeal.

Even so, he'd briefly considered seeking a third opinion, before the folly of it settled like ashes over him in a belated awareness that it was only the doctor's curt, pompous demeanor—his near-tone-deaf absence of any bedside manner—that had made him rebel. The realization had left him even less able to challenge the unhedged death sentence. Only a physician whose diagnostic skills were as acute as this patrician Brit's could afford to pay so little attention to his patients' feelings—have the preening arrogance to liken the disease's lightning course to Hitler's panzers pouring across Poland. Respond to every question with a clipped chorus of in *point of facts* and *quite sos*.

Perhaps if he had seen him earlier, even a "fortnight or two" earlier, things might have been different. Still "more than a bit dodgy, doubtless," but an outside chance. Now, there was none. Again the dark irony registered. He was an old man, past seventy, but the disease was coursing through his shrunken body as if he had the hyperactive metabolism of a teenage boy. Any conceivable treatment, he had been all too bluntly "given to understand," had not the remotest chance of controlling, much less stopping, its relentless advance.

But this last day on a trout stream, this at least, he could control. The first glints of dawn showed through the clouds in the eastern sky as he pulled up to the drive-in window of a local coffee house, opened his glove box, and spread the dog-eared map across the steering wheel as his latte was being prepared. *Trout Streams of Southeastern Minnesota.* This too, like the streamers, he hadn't used for some time—had kept only because it had once been so useful to him. *Winnebago. Rush Creek. Trout Run.* Through the passing decades he had fished them all, come to know them all, each of them far better than the little brook he was heading for now. He hadn't walked its meadow banks in close to thirty years. Checking the warren of connecting township roads a final time, he paid for his coffee, refolded the map, and drove out of town in the early morning light.

The first symptoms had appeared barely four months earlier, and he dismissed them as the flu. Then came two or three days of headaches and nausea a few weeks later—late May? early June?—but again he had recovered and thought little of it, had in fact felt good enough to keep his annual rendezvous with an old college friend for the green drake hatch on the Henrys Fork in Idaho, where for once they'd hit the dates right and caught more large trout than he could count. He hadn't seen his doctor until the first week of August, at least two weeks after the symptoms returned and swelled into a stomach-churning nausea that didn't abate. He grew worried that the engorged deer tick he'd found in his crotch hair two days after he'd killed a wild turkey in April had infected him with Lyme disease.

As he drove on, the stream of memory dredged up a story by Tolstoy, *The Death of Ivan Ilych,* about a self-absorbed striver not unlike himself, preoccupied with the petty details of living until the day he learns he's been stricken with a fatal disease. He rarely read literature, but this story had lodged in his subconscious like that bloated deer tick from as far back as his freshman English class at Cornell. *There's a divinity that shapes our ends, rough-hew them how we will.* Yet another mocking echo that had stuck, from where or when he no longer knew.

But there would be no more anger, tears. Not at least on this day. He'd risen early enough to beat the heavy rain that was forecast for early in the afternoon, and he remained confident—if his memories from all those years ago were trustworthy—that even in his weakened state he could fish the little brook from the grassy meadow, where the gravel road reached it, all the way up to the pebbly runs and riffles near its source. How much stream would that be to negotiate? A half-mile? Three-quarters? In his current condition it would have been unthinkable to breast the hard-flowing current of bigger water, but there would be no such challenge here. In memory, the brook's deepest pools were barely thigh-deep—slow moving pockets beneath overhung rocks, easily skirted—its grade gradual until it climbed abruptly up to the spring that flowed out of a limestone outcrop below a ridge. There were only native brook trout there, or so it had been on that spring day so many years ago when he'd first fished it. Exploring the foreign hinterlands in his car, a couple of weeks after IBM had convinced him to relocate from New York with a promotion and higher salary, he'd happened on the stream by pure chance. A more experienced eye—his own eye, even a couple of years later—would have viewed it as merely passable trout water, hardly a stretch to quicken an angler's pulse. But in that rapturous moment of discovery, rounding a downhill bend in the gravel road and catching the diamond glint of a riffle through the windshield, his heart had leapt. It was unmistakably a trout stream, in a part of America the endless corn and soybean fields had almost convinced him couldn't possibly hold any. The fact had registered instantly, and he knew he'd return a day or two later, fly rod in hand.

The first fish had flashed at a Micky Finn streamer. A fat ten- or eleven-inch brown that he killed and gutted to cook and eat in his still mostly unfurnished apartment that night. A few hundred yards farther on he'd switched to nymphs, with no success, still so inexperienced in how to fish them he could recognize only the most aggressive strikes. Farther up, where wooded bluffs rose in a sharp angle above him, he'd seen a rise and switched instantly to a Henryville Special—caught three or four of the bright, celestially hued brookies that had sealed that May morning in a nostalgic memory as fresh as the handful of morel mushrooms he'd stumbled on hiking euphorically back to his car.

He reached the stream as the late August sun broke over a bluff to the east, turning a clump of sumac just up the road a garish crimson. Parking beside it, he strung the rod and spread-eagled the sagging barbed-wire fence, his chest heaving from the effort as he plodded a few steps on across the spongy meadow grass. It was already clear that his decision not to wear waders was the right one. Lying in bed, unable to sleep with pain and anticipation, he'd had ample time to plan every detail—decided to further re-create that vanished day from his youth by wading wet in a pair of worn sneakers and faded jeans. In the blind naïveté of the moment he hadn't considered the expense of energy—how the lighter garb would also help husband his diminished reserves of strength. Unzipping the vest, he removed the water bottle from its back pocket and poured all but a few sips onto the ground. It was fortunate he had left nearly everything else at home—emptied the vest of virtually all but the single fly box and a pair of tippet spools.

Reaching the brook, he paused only long enough to steady his breathing and tie on one of the streamers—took a longer moment to gaze at the thigh-deep pool that flowed beneath some overhanging tree roots on the opposite bank. Thick beds of watercress cloaked the gravelly flanks where the riffle flowed into it, narrowing the throat to little more than a foot. The sun-splashed water above the shadowed pool was even clearer than he remembered, literally as pellucid as a glass of cold gin.

He caught a sleek brown on his second cast, working the streamer slowly past the overhanging tangle of roots, and then a second, slightly larger trout a few casts later. The current was cold as ice on his hands as he released them. Shuffling upstream through the riffle he paused to wipe the sweat off his forehead, then snipped off the fly and replaced it with a smaller one, a Bead-Head Prince.

His feet felt briefly lighter. These were things he *could* control. He moved on toward the little brook's source, the flies he continued to change ever smaller, his legs numbing in the frigid water as if for a transcendent two or three hours his life had frozen back in the stream of time. His hands had long ago learned to sense the subtle take of a nymph that the stronger hands of his youth had failed to recognize, and he caught and released four more trout before reaching the meadow's end.

He struggled over a second strand of barbed wire and fished on. Over the verdant ridge to the south he caught the sudden flash of lightning—heard the heavy drumroll of thunder echo seconds later off the bluffs. He switched impulsively to a small Adams though he had not yet seen a single fish rise. The rain would come sooner than forecast, that was obvious, but what did it matter. Yet another dark irony. Thoughts of exposure to lightning that had made him cower in his youth held no fear for him now. By the time the first droplets spattered the yellowing leaves of a streamside poplar, two trout had risen to the dry fly and been brought to hand.

He labored to quicken his own pace as the rain abruptly quickened, soaking his clothes and forcing a change of the now useless fly. Shaking from the cold, he struggled to attach the tiniest nymph in his box to the leader tippet, peering at it through bleared glasses beneath the dripping bill of his cap. A stiff wind had risen, riding the advancing storm, and he felt the little four-weight rod stiffen against it as he forced the tiny fly to bore upstream through the heavy air. The effort was nearly all he could muster in his enfeebled arm. When the small trout struck and flashed in the water he was sure it was a brookie—felt his heart soar higher as the dappled sides flashed again beneath the tightened line and he pulled it flopping onto the grass. Holding it in the palm of his trembling hand he stared at it through the blur of his glasses, the last fish he would ever catch, its incandescent colors magnified by the raindrops. A brook trout like the first he had ever caught, in virtually the same place, almost forty years before.

On his knees he held the fish a moment longer in the current, already visibly rising and stained with streaks of mud—held it until the silvery skin quivered and the fish was gone. Standing, he lifted the rod off the grass and took what little shelter he could find under a nearby pine tree, waiting for the storm to pass. In less than ten minutes the little brook had turned unfishable, silt-choked rivulets draining down the adjacent hillsides whose once-stabilizing hardwoods had been clear cut years before. A feeder spring a hundred yards downstream, narrow enough he had stepped across it barely a half-hour earlier, was now a knee-deep torrent. The placid pool just below it where he'd caught a good brown on the Adams had become a menacing, chocolate-colored swirl of indeterminate depth.

And still it rained, rained still harder, as if the skies had opened and the gods were pouring a cauldron of unleashed fury onto the land. It was astonishing, how quickly the storm had come on—how much the brook had changed.

Through the squall he could barely make out the upper end of the meadow, fewer than two hundred yards below him—saw that cascades of water were sluicing violently down across it from the surrounding bluffs. It was clear he had waited too long to return to the car—could not possibly make his way back now the way he had come. Even here, not far from the source, the stream had risen so high he could no longer safely have crossed it.

Peering upstream into the slanting rain, at the deepening troughs the runoff was carving into the overgrazed hillsides, he was struck with the realization that even where he crouched the ground would not remain unflooded for long.

Again he felt no fear, felt instead a sharpening of the senses that was briefly euphoric before flattening out into a kind of preternatural calm. Rising from beneath the sodden tree he took stock of his situation. His soaked body was shaking violently from the cold; his feet were numb; within minutes, if he didn't forge on to the higher ground upstream, it would be too late. Lifting the little fly rod off the soggy grass, he left the tree's scant shelter and staggered farther on up the coulee, his shoes slipping with each forced step he took into the full fury of the storm.

The narrow patch of ground he finally reached rose only a few inches above the swelling stream, but he could go no farther. On drier earth he might have been able to climb the steep incline to a limestone shelf ten feet above him, but the ascent was impossible now in the grease-slick mud. There was nowhere else to go. Again the hard truth swept through him without fear or panic. He must somehow reach the safety of the rocky outcrop, or soon be swept away by the currents already lapping at his shoes.

Something sharp stung his cheek and he swiped at it, peered more intently into the storm. Just beyond the rock ledge the limb of a slanted pine tree extended several feet over the water, shedding needles like tiny darts with every savage gust of wind. Was there any way to anchor to it—*pull* himself up to the shelf? He stared down at the rod in his trembling hand, knew the idea forming in his brain was close to absurd but his only chance.

Unclipping the knife attached to his vest, the fisherman unspooled line off his reel and pulled it down through the bending rod until he held the thick butt end of the leader, a foot below the nail knot that spliced it to the line. With a swift slash of the blade he severed it, then unzipped the pocket of his vest and fumbled to remove the three big streamers. The brightest was the fly he had caught the first fish on, less than two hours earlier. The fact seemed inconceivable now.

Shaking almost uncontrollably in the cold, he worked to steady his hands and his vision enough to thread the stiff butt through the eyes of the three hooks, then struggled harder to knot them with his cramping fingers. When at last the flies were secured, he bound them tighter together with several turns of the discarded leader he'd held in his chattering teeth. Stripping line down off the reel, he felt his fingers tighten on the rod handle, had the grim, fleeting thought that the term *death grip* was not simply a metaphor.

The pine bough yawed toward him in the horizontal sheets of rain pelting his face, at least fifteen sloped feet above him. The timing would have to be perfect. The line would need to recoil off the loaded rod with such force the flies would burrow like a fletched arrow through the howling wind. Did enough strength remain in his arm to do it? Taking a long breath, he tried to visualize it—force his mind to the focus he had once summoned in what was probably the single best cast of his life, dropping a tiny Blue Wing Olive above a huge brown feeding in a Montana spring creek that was so sunlit and glassy it seemed impossible not to send the fish rocketing to safety deep in the pool. He had caught that trout, the largest of his life.

Charged with the memory, he lifted the rod in a single abrupt backcast and threw the bound flies forward with a violent snap of his arthritic wrist into the storm. In the driving rain, he didn't see them clear the bough and blow instantly back beneath it—saw only the tightening of the line as he drew back hard and felt the anchored tug at its end.

He lay the rod down only long enough to remove his shoes and socks—dig his naked toes as deeply as he could into the base of the mud-slick incline that rose above him. Looping several coils of slack line around the rod handle to secure it, he took a single tentative step. Pulled his body eight or ten inches upward. The line throbbed like taut wire through the rod guides, but it held. Securing the gain with more loops around the handle he advanced another few inches, then a few inches more . . .

The following spring a college student pulled his motorcycle off on the shoulder of the gravel road, lifted his spinning rod and canvas creel off the rack behind him, and loped down across the talus slope to the stream. He had never been here before—had fished for trout only two or three times in his young life—but the couple of small fish he'd managed to catch had excited him enough he'd impulsively decided to cut his chemistry class and find one of the streams marked on his new map, *Trout Streams of Southeastern Minnesota*. He couldn't tell if this one was good or bad, knew only that the April afternoon was totally primo and he had a couple of cold beers in his backpack—could build a fire if he was lucky enough to catch a fish, cook it right there on the shore. The land wasn't posted, and there were so many dead branches and fallen trees on the debris-strewn shoreline it looked like an earthquake had struck it. He'd still been back home in Chicago, at the end of summer vacation, when the big flood hit the previous summer. But you could see the devastation wherever you looked. People said almost eighteen inches of rain had fallen in less than twenty-four hours. Newspaper stories described it as an *apocalyptic* storm.

That seemed excessive to him, but the land beside the stream did look something like a lunar landscape, nothing but rocks and the tangles of broken tree limbs and a few chunks of twisted sheet metal that were probably a swept-away shed or grain bin but now resembled some wrecked module from outer space. Even the scoured stream looked slightly surreal, and he wondered if any fish remained in it. But hell, he thought, they all looked that way now, after the flood, and the guy in the bait shop where he'd bought his night crawlers had said this one would probably be as good as any. It had always been decent before, the guy said, as far as he knew, and it never got much fishing pressure. Not very often, anyway. Some old dude had actually drowned fishing it the day of the storm, the guy had added with a grim laugh, shaking his head. "Hard to believe, ain't it—that he'd stay out there in the rain long enough to be swept away? They found his body a day or two later, tangled in some tree roots down by the Iowa border. His pants and shoes and socks were gone but he still had his fishing vest on."

Threading a crawler on the treble hook of his spinner, the student made a half dozen fruitless casts into the elbow pool where he'd reached the stream, then walked on. Moving swiftly, he'd fished several more riffles and flood-carved pools without success when the trout hit—a fat, fourteen-inch rainbow that struck the silver spinner as it spun past a submerged tree trunk and bulled upstream against the current before the youth finally managed to drag it onto the gravel shore. Yelping with delight he seized it—felt the hardness of its body quiver in his hand. He had gutted it and slipped the fish into his creel, sat on the sand sipping a celebratory beer, when the glint of something metallic caught his eye in the noonday sun.

He set the beer can on a rock and loped over to it—a disc of tarnished metal half-buried in the mud. Running a finger around it he saw at once that it was a fly reel, still attached to a rod completely covered by the sand and muck-crusted debris. Yet when he pawed the mud away he found the rod miraculously intact, and he carried it back to the water. The scoured stream was as clear as crystal, seemed totally devoid of any bottom mud or vegetation. It stained only briefly even when he submerged the clotted reel and rod in it again and again, washing them clean. When all visible trace of grime was gone, he gave the reel a tentative crank—cringed at the sound of the sand grinding in its gears but felt the spool turn and saw a loose coil of line go taut beneath his hand.

Other coils were looped tight around the rod handle—it was totally weird what a flood could do, wrapping them that tightly—and his eyes drifted down the line past the tip of the rod. For the first time he noticed that something was tied at its end. Rising, he walked up the stream bank to where it lay on the sand. The mud-coated lure at his feet bewildered him. Rinsing it too in the stream, he was still more bewildered, even stunned. The weird rig he held now in his palm was like nothing he'd ever seen before, even in a fishing magazine. Three wet-feathered flies, the hooks broken off two of them, were wrapped side by side and tied together by a short length of thick leader. The barb of the single hook that remained was embedded in a little piece of wood that looked like bark from a spruce or a pine.

He hadn't had much fishing experience, but he couldn't imagine that this setup could be effective—fool something as wily as a trout, or even a sucker or carp for that matter. Fool *any* fish with eyes and half a brain. But what the fuck did he know about fly fishing?

I'll be damned, he said audibly to himself. He'd have to show it to the dude in the bait shop, see what he made of it. Picking his beer up and taking a long, satisfying swig, he leaned the fly rod against a rock. He'd pick it up on his way back downstream.

His eyes on the clear pool ahead of him, the youth fished on.

Coachmen

It was a Saturday morning in February when the telephone rang as I was chipping ice off my doorstep. Dropping the shovel, I shucked my Sorels and padded inside to answer it.

"C'gradulations, ol' buddy," the caller drawled. "You've just been picked by the Root Valley Reelmen. Fourth round of the 'naugural Cat Draft."

It took a second to recognize the voice.

"Floyd?" I said.

"You better believe it, chief," he answered. "Get your tail on down here to draft headquarters so we can get a jump on this thang."

I didn't have any idea what he was talking about. Floyd was a CPA, a tax consultant. But ever since he'd started watching *Bassmaster Classics* he'd gone off the deep end trying to become a fishing celebrity on TV. I couldn't get a handle on him. There was only one thing I was sure of—he wasn't likely to take no for an answer. I resigned myself and let him go on.

"Where are you calling from?" I asked. "Who are the Root Valley Reelmen?"

"Just get yourself on down here to the Gutter Bowl," he finished. "We'll fill you in. When they write the book on trout fishing in America, you're gonna be on the cutting edge."

The snowplows still hadn't cleared the parking lot when I got to the bowling alley an hour later, so I parked on the street near the front door. Inside the lounge, Floyd sat at one of the booths with a hulking young guy I'd never seen before. A tagboard chart was taped to the wall behind his head.

"Come on over here, Bubba," he shouted, as my eyes adjusted to the smoky light. "This big hooter's my assistant, Duke Dettle. We took him number two in the draft."

The stranger extracted himself from the booth and stood bulkily above me, his arms bulging out of a T-shirt like a pair of smoked hams. "Reelmen" was logoed across the shirt's front.

"Makes you wonder who went number one," I murmured, adding a smile lest the big hooter take offense. Behind me a bowling ball rumbled down the alley, clunked against a single pin.

"Number one's me," Floyd finally offered, clearing his throat. "I founded both the league and our franchise, so there wadn't nobody logical to take as numero uno but myself. But hey, that don't make no never mind," he added, slapping me on the shoulder. "There ain't no I in team. Let's start talkin' *trout!*"

"I'm still confused," I answered. "What league are we talking about?"

"The CATT," he said, stabbing his finger at the wall chart. "Competitive Anglers for Tournament Trout."

"You're planning to fish for trout in *competition?*" I stared at him. It felt like sacrilege—on a par with holding a poker tournament in the cathedral at Chartres. I wasn't sure I'd heard him right.

"You bet," he responded. "You gotta get tuned into the twenty-first century, Bubba. Tournament fishin's hot. I know it's your first day as a Reelman, but hey, don't you ever turn on your tube?"

"I've been shoveling snow," I said defensively. "I've got a lot of snow over at my place."

"We got a little snow now, sure," he muttered, "just like ever' February. That means the season opener's only six weeks off. If we don't get started on some winter conditioning, Fox River's gonna kick our butt."

"Fox River?" I said, even more bewildered at this mention of a tiny burg about ten miles up the valley road.

"You got it," he fired back. "The Fox River Ferrule Dogs. Right now they're the league's only other franchise, so we're gonna see a lot of their rods come spring. Word is they throw a real tight line and get after you right from the get-go. And they know how to hit that open hole."

"I'm still confused," I said. "You're talking about fishing for *trout?*"

He stared at me for five or ten seconds, shaking his head.

"Duke's checked 'em out," he finally continued. "They're tougher 'n boiled owl. But that don't mean we're ready to call the hounds in. What I hear, they got some line problems, and their tackle's gettin' old. We go out there and fish like I think we can in the opener, we got 'em where the hair gets shor—"

"Are you telling me," I interrupted him, "that they're the only other *franchise* you've got?"

"Charter members," he grinned. "Just like us. We're workin' on another one up on Chicken Ridge, but it's gonna be awhile yet before the Hackleheads are ready. A man can't fish in this league just because he knows about line backing and what fly patterns are all about. Even if he's got the want-to. It's got to *mean* something to be a Hacklehead or a Reelman."

He stared at me as if I'd turned down a week on the best water in New Zealand for an hour of dunking doughballs for carp.

"It's probably great even if you're a Ferrule Dog," I added. "I just don't see what—"

"Listen up," he said. "It's simple. The only thang you gotta do between now and the season opener is get those wheels of yours back in shape. You'll be our number four rod," he added, "after me and Duke and the old guy."

"The old guy?" I said.

"Right. He'll be down later for the video. Duke says he's a little long in the tooth, but you gotta love the way he gets after 'em when he hits the water. He'll do us some good."

"The *video?*"

"It's back in the film room," Floyd answered, twitching his shoulder toward a large broom closet. "The Duke's been out on Crooked Creek and got us some scoutin' shots. It's not against the rules. Come opening day, we're gonna have good reads on ever' hole—hit those Dogs with a game plan you wouldn't believe. It's gotta get their dauber down."

"Are you serious about all this?" I blurted, still numbed by this latest transformation from the old Floyd. "I mean, what are *the rules*? How do you know who's won or lost?"

"Catch and release," he fired back at once. "Total inches takes the big enchilada. But you gotta have visual proof with your cell phone or a digital camera. No fish scores unless you got a shot of him laid out flatside against a ruler. Ten-inch penalty for jumping the seven o'clock starting whistle. Fifteen-inch for encroachment on another man's hole."

"Who decides where you fish?" I plunged on. If a reeling brain made you a Reelman, I should have been the number one pick. "What if everybody heads for the Rockface Pool?"

He glanced around nervously, then bent closer, lowering his voice.

"Speed, Bubba," he whispered. "It's the name of the game. Speed kills. Hit that hole first, it's yours as long as you wanna fish it. That's why we made you our pick."

"I don't know," I said dubiously. "Not too many guys run well in hippers, and in April you can't wade wet."

"You got it," he said, winking. "That's the kind o' thinkin' we're countin' on from the Ferrule Dogs. When we come out for that opening whistle, what's it gonna do to their want-to when they see us wearin' these?"

Glancing over his shoulder like a felon about to stuff a scribbled note through a bank teller's window, he reached under the table and pulled out a large box. Inside were four pairs of green neoprene waders. *REELMEN* was printed in orange block letters across the seats.

"You're going to wear those?" I blurted.

"Where the hell you been, Ernie?" he countered. "I swear, some-times it's like you caught some train back to the 1950s. Don't you ever read your Orvis catalog? Put on a pair of these things, you're gonna hit that hole a helluva lot quicker. I don't care if you have lost a step or two."

"I don't see how I can help you," I said honestly. "All this is a whole lot different from the way I've always fished."

"You've got some work to do, sure," he answered. "Just like ever'body else in the preseason. I've got to start some weightin' work on my Woolly Buggers myself. Don't worry 'bout it. Duke's got it all down on your chart."

"My *chart?*"

"Sure. The stats, the poop—how you're gonna match up out there, skillwise, ever' Sunday. Here, Duke can explain it. I gotta take a leak."

He tossed me his clipboard and shuffled across the carpet toward the men's room, looking a little dazed.

"Let's see what Coach's got," the Duke mumbled, taking the clipboard from me. "He's the one that did your scouting report."

"*Coach?*" I said distractedly, still awed by the bulge of the big hooter's biceps. "You call Floyd *Coach?*"

The Duke didn't say anything for a moment, chewing slowly on a plastic toothpick. Then he shook his head and looked down at the clipboard, began to read.

"Let's start with your strengths," he began, "the stuff you can do to help us." He paused again, glancing down at my puffy insulated pants and Sorels, and read on. "Says here you've still got decent wheels," he mumbled dubiously. "Coach says you get to a hole about as quick after some other fisherman's left it as anybody he's ever seen."

"Floyd already told me that," I said.

"Okay," he answered, looking up from the clipboard. "Let's move on to where you're weak." Blinking slowly and hunching what was either his neck or the beginning of his shoulders, he stared at me like a sea tortoise eyeing an overweight crab. I didn't ask him if I had any other strengths.

"First thing is how you handle the pressure," he went on. "The days when they're really hitting. Coach says you can take the small ones for hours, but tend to clutch up when the big ones start hittin' hard."

"The hard hits always surprise you," I admitted, reddening. "But over the years I've taken as many good ones as Floyd."

He paused for a moment, gnawing on the toothpick, then went on.

"Your fly patterns," he said. "They're stale—have got too dry and predictable. Coach says you go deep about as often as tits show up on a boar."

123

"What about Floyd?" I protested. "*Coach*. Talk about stale. A weighted Woolly Bugger is all he ever uses. He goes deep every time he picks up his rod."

The Duke looked up, slowly lifted a ballpoint pen from the table, and wrote "Attitude" on the clipboard beside my name.

"Gizzard," he went on, his jaw tightening. "Gizzardwise, you're just not gettin' it done. You gotta get after 'em out there, even on those days it's muddy or windy or your hands are numbin' up in the snow."

"I don't like to fish with pain," I confessed. "I head for home when I'm cold and hungry. Face it, I'm not the kind of guy you can use."

"Cowboy up," he countered, biting down harder on the toothpick. "Take one for the team. Even if you can't catch nothing, we can always use you to block."

"Block?" I said.

"Right. Think about it. The Dogs'll have their eye on the Rockface Pool, like you said, but we use your wheels to lock it up at the opening whistle. Then Coach and me and the old guy take over and really start to kick some—"

"Wait a minute," I cut him off. "Is that the reason Floyd—"

"Hold on," he stopped me, lifting a meaty hand as he turned his head. "I think the old guy just got here. Looks like he just came in off the lake."

I turned toward the door, where someone about five feet three stood hunched in baggy wool pants and a dirty Packers sweatshirt. A checkered cap with earflaps perched on his gray head.

"The *Geezer*?" I said. "He's the old guy Floyd was talking about?"

"You know him?"

"I went out on the ice with him once," I said. "The Geezer's your number three pick? Floyd thinks the *Geezer* fishes flies?" I stared back toward the door in disbelief. He was a little older, but unmistakably the same crusty old coot who'd frozen me half to death the only time I'd ever been fool enough to go ice fishing. The same old dude who told me his car heater was "on the fritzer" and muttered, when I complained about the wind chill, "Dat always gets me, da big deal dey make about da vind-shill. Who da hell tinks about vind ven dere's good *ice?*"

I glanced back at the Duke, who looked as uncomfortable as I was bewildered.

"Not flies," he answered, coloring. "Bait. Every team in the league gets one designated Baiter. The old guy's old—no way you can get around that—but we're bettin' he can still get the job done, baitwise." Hollering, he waved the Geezer over to our table. I tried to look non-chalant as he approached.

"Dem sunnies are hittin', hey," he croaked, unzipping his sweat-shirt. "You boys oughta been out dere dis morning about six."

"I don't go out on the ice anymore," the Duke responded. "Not since Coach taught me what fly fishing is all about."

"Dat's a mistake," the Geezer grunted. "Dat's a big mistake." He shook his head, then peered at me as he reached in his pocket for a chaw of Red Man. I pulled my coat collar up a little higher. He didn't seem to recognize my face.

"Coach is back," the Duke announced as Floyd loped across the carpet toward us, his hand stretching out to welcome his number three rod.

"Big guy!" he shouted. "Great to have you on the Reelmen! I got a feelin' you're gonna go out there and really lay some heavy hittin' on 'em—put some kind o' numbers on the board."

The Geezer looked at Floyd like a man who's answered the doorbell expecting a pizza and found a Jehovah's Witness grinning on his step.

"You're da guy dat called me dis morning when I vas cleanin' fish?" he said.

"Good to meet ya," Floyd answered. "Duke tells me you're one pure-dee kind o' garden hackler. He says watchin' you work the chub-and-crawler option beats killin' snakes with a stick."

"I come down here for dat draft, hey," the Geezer ignored him, jerking his arm in the direction of the bar taps. "You said dis is vere I'd meet da real men in da valley and get four good rounds of brew."

"Brew? What brew?" Floyd said, his brow furrowing.

"I don't know, hey. Over da phone it sounded like *Noggle Cat* draft, but dat's some new brand I ain't never heard of. Say," he added, his eyes narrowing beneath his bushy brows, "is dis some trick—one o' dem pyr'mid tings I been hearin' about lately?"

Floyd was still trying to explain it all to him when I saw my chance and ducked out the side door. "Hittin' that open hole, Bubba," I murmured, glancing back at him as the door swung shut behind me. "It's the name of the game."

Indian Summer

He lurched down the lane in a euphoric daze, half-blinded by the October light. Fumbling in his vest for his sunglasses, he was a hundred yards from his car before the torn, empty pockets registered and he paused, shaking his head.

"Christ," he mumbled. "Back off a little. You've got a couple of hours. You've got time."

He moved on down the rutted lane between rows of corn, his slowed gait now wildly out of sync with his still racing heartbeat. The fiberglass rod trembled in his fingers. The tattered vest rode weightless on his sweat-dampened shirt.

He was reveling in the warmth, his pulse finally quieting, when a sudden explosion near his shoes spooked him into a panicked sidestep. A cock pheasant rocketed through the rattle of corn leaves, cackling wildly, then flared and soared on over the tassels, its tail streaming against the azure sky.

It was too much, all of it. One more surreal blaze of color on a brain already sated with hues splashed like hallucinogens on the wooded hills. He paused again, laughing, tried to idle down the flood of feeling that filled his chest. The undersize vest rose and fell over his stomach, its empty, mutilated pockets gaping wide.

Reflexively, he patted the one whose zipper had somehow remained intact, checking for the pill bottle into which, an hour earlier, he'd dropped the half-dozen worn flies he'd gratefully plucked from the vest's scruffy wool patch.

He glanced at his watch, then down at his shoes, their loose canvas sides flopping the way both his kids had ten or twelve years earlier, back in the '80s. The way a few of his students' shoes still did, he realized, though that craze seemed largely to have played itself out. Occasionally, peering out from behind his lectern, he'd still see the odd pair or two—torn, unlaced sneakers like the ones Mike had left on the floor of his room when he went off to Dartmouth. But not often. A more straitlaced look was clearly back in fashion. At least among the nose-to-the-grindstone types that filled most of his classroom seats now.

The thin rubber soles squished on, sliding through the mud, and again he snorted with laughter, tickled by the incongruity. Would any of them believe it, this metamorphosis—their button-down prof schlepping along like a hobo about to jump a slow freight? But the old pair of Keds were all he could find in the dusty recesses of his office closet, hanging beside the too-tight sweatsuit he'd also snatched impulsively off the hook and tugged on. The ragtag vest had been there too, last used to sop up a spilled pot of coffee. And miraculously, mercifully—shoved even farther back on the shelf where it had sat gathering dust ever since he'd bought his son his first graphite—the long-forgotten little rod with the cracked line and dinged reel.

It felt like stealing watermelons, the pure, boyish pleasure of it. Had felt like it from the moment he first realized he might actually be able to pull the caper off. He had no idea whether the bedraggled flies could entice a fish. Or whether the frayed tippet would hold at the end of the ossified leader. None of it mattered. It was the last day of the season. And in a confluence of events as serendipitous as this bizarre, stunning alchemy in the weather, he was going to spend its last precious hours fishing for trout.

He justified it to himself as a kind of divinely sanctioned delinquency, like Mardi Gras or the Feast of Fools. A license to steal.

Two days before, the season's last Sunday, he'd come off Rush Creek soaking wet, chilled, and nearly fishless after six hours of hammering a Woolly Worm through a lowering sky the color of asphalt. He'd driven home through the fall's first sting of snowflakes, then glumly cleaned and packed his gear away for the year.

Hell, that very morning, only a few hours earlier, the frosted lawn outside his bedroom window had been blanketed in chill fog.

But the sun had burned it off as he and his wife ate breakfast, then had kept on burning a golden hole in the sky. It was as if a window of grace had suddenly opened. By the time he walked across the quad to his noon class, the transformation was so complete it struck him as weirdly sacramental. Rock music blared from dorm windows. Frisbees soared and hovered. Glistening, near-naked bodies lazed on lawns and dorm balconies like drowsing seals.

When his atypically boisterous class began cajoling him to abandon the lecture hall for the clipped, grassy slope beside the chemistry building, he'd finally said to hell with it and given in.

It was the first of what soon became a chain of such yieldings. Or perhaps *sheddings* was more accurate, it occurred to him now, as he shuffled on down the muddy lane through the corn. First his lecture notes. Then his coat and tie. Finally what was left of his professional inhibitions. The last nuzzling pair of students had barely drifted away toward the arboretum when he was back in the classroom, taping the hastily scrawled note to the door.

Professor Quinn is ill today. His one o'clock seminar will not meet this afternoon.

He didn't expect anybody to believe it, student or colleague. But that didn't matter either. The spirit of carnival seemed so pervasive he couldn't imagine anyone but old maids of both sexes too untouched or uptight to care.

He glanced again at his watch, slowed abruptly, and suddenly remembered the weeping girl he'd promised to meet at two thirty to discuss her failed midterm exam. "Damn," he muttered, recalling her tear-stained face. Why the hell hadn't he thought to tape the same note to his office door?

For a moment he considered turning back—driving the couple of miles back to the Kwik-Trip on the highway and calling the department secretary to have her get in touch with the girl. The impulse died as quickly as it sprang. He'd already walked several hundred yards from the car; the girl had missed at least half a dozen classes; and the days were short enough now, the stream far enough down in the ridge-shaded valley, darkness would fall not much later than five. He'd fished the pool only once before in his life, a couple of years earlier with Dooley, and if his memory was accurate its tree-shrouded banks lay close to a mile from where he was parked.

He'd call the girl's dorm when he got home, he promised himself—do what he could within the bounds of professional ethics to give her a break.

It had long since become clear to him that he could have driven the field lane—needn't have parked back by the highway. The occasional puddles he passed were negotiable and the lane was grassy, packed firm beneath the surface mud. The tire tracks ahead of him were recent enough, in fact, they might have been made only a few minutes before.

He closed his eyes briefly, praying they hadn't been. Normally it wouldn't have bothered him much. He even expected it, another fisher or two out on a day as magnificent as this. You simply moved on until you were clear of them. It was one of the best things about trout fishing—that mobility—one of the biggest reasons he'd never taken much to fishing from a boat. You remained trapped there even if it moved. But on a trout stream, you just kept walking until you were free of other anglers. He'd always believed in sharing the wealth.

Yet this stream was different, different enough he'd never been back to it, despite the fact it was much closer to town than any of his favorite haunts. For though the pool Dooley had put him on was both gin clear and accessible, from what he'd seen it was the only stretch of water worth fishing for some distance beyond.

True, it was big enough for two. Casting from opposite banks, he and Dooley had taken fish there together, including a heavy-bodied eighteen-incher his friend had teased with a streamer from an undercut pine. But it hadn't been enough to tempt him back until today, when the stream's proximity to town was all he required. In the shank hours that remained of the season, a single good pool would be enough.

It would, at least, if no one else was standing in it.

Pausing to bend closer over the tire tracks, he felt his chest tighten. He'd barely noticed them at first, back up by the road, where they were gouged so deeply into the mud he'd assumed they'd been made by a tractor. But it was clear now that they hadn't been—were the tracks of a car or a pickup—an indistinct set that momentarily diverged into two shallower sets skirting a pothole before fusing again a few feet farther on. He breathed easier, noticing this, felt almost certain it meant a single vehicle had tracked back out after driving in.

Fifty yards ahead the field lane angled sharply left along the fenceline and he could see the land fall away into the densely wooded coulee beyond. If he remembered, the winding trail down to the stream took another eight or ten minutes. The pool lay a couple of hundred yards farther on, just upstream of the first bend.

He felt the quickening again in his loins, the primal stirring—that adrenaline rush in the presence of running water that seemed only to intensify as he slid into the first declines of age. He could hear his own breath, faintly wheezing. The shards of sunlight piercing the corn tassels made his eyes start to swim.

Pausing just short of the fence, he was fumbling for his handkerchief, his chest laboring, when a glint of metal flickered incongruously through the last rows of cornstalks. His heart sank as he brushed a dry leaf aside and felt his fear confirmed. A car sat parked around the bend in the lane.

A few more dispirited steps and he reached the fence, saw the black Isuzu, knew at once what he'd find when he arrived at the stream. Dooley. The Vikings decal on the rear bumper was as unmistakable as the dent above the tailpipe, unrepaired since they'd backed into a rock down on Winnebago several weeks before.

For a moment anger welled in his throat, a sense of betrayal, primal as that of the first Neanderthal who parted the leaves on his favorite water hole only to find another hunter's heavy footprint in the sand. The resentment ebbed to disappointment only with a grudging self-reminder that it had been Dooley who'd revealed the pool to him in the first place—that his own words had been even more emphatic, a day earlier, when the two of them had finished their weekly squash session at the Y:

"I hear it's gonna be nice tomorrow."

131

"And I've got two afternoon classes. No matter how nice it is, I'm screwed."

"Same damn thing last year, when it closed on that bluebird Monday. Problem with God is he's a bait-dunker. Or maybe he just doesn't know how to dance—got your basic piss-poor sense of rhythm. Every closing weekend I can remember, I had to thaw my friggin' balls out before I could pack away my gear."

He'd broken up at that, despite their shared frustration. One thing about Dooley, he was always good for a laugh.

The van sat only a few yards ahead of him as he turned and plodded on between the fence and the corn. His eyes were drifting past it, on to the trailhead, when a shadow suddenly flickered through the rear glass.

He stopped. Looked again. Caught again the bob of a head through the hard glare off the window.

"So the bastard just got here himself," he murmured, happy in the knowledge he wouldn't have to horn in on him at the pool. "Hasn't even had time to change his clothes."

Shielding his eyes from the glaring sun, he was about to walk on— call out—his lips forming "Dool, you wily old fox, what'd you do—tell everybody in the office your grandmother kicked the bucket?"

The pale limb rose through a wink of sunlight that closed as quickly as it had opened, as fleeting but unequivocal as a fly snatched below a riffle's glittering sheen. *A woman's leg. Long and naked.* Behind the dappled glass, it swam surreally in his eyes like a fun-house mirror.

Stunned, he ducked back into the corn, the dry leaves brushing sharply across his face, his sneakered feet sliding over a muddy furrow. Three rows in, he stopped, his brain cartwheeling over what he should do. Sweat trickled down his nose. A gray worm inched up a cornstalk. A flock of starlings dipped and disintegrated in the sky above him, came apart like ashes scattering in the wind.

He'd known that Dooley was unfaithful, had an eye for women. Sensed that they liked him. Didn't find it hard to believe that the old tailback's slope-shouldered body still held enough spring to attract them. What did it matter? Let him have his fun. God knows he'd had plenty of his own, surrounded every day of his working life by nubile young women in their sexual prime. There was nothing to do but slip past as quietly as he could—move on to the trailhead that led down to the stream. *What the hell*, it suddenly occurred to him. Why draw any conclusions? Maybe it wasn't another woman. Maybe it was Annie, the guy's own leggy wife.

Creeping as noiselessly as he could down the row, he shot a last glance toward the lane—found himself staring straight into the van's half-open sliding door. He heard a moan. Then another. Saw a lacy pair of panties dangling over the front seat. The blow to his stomach nearly brought him to his knees.

Even from where he stood, ten yards away, the tiny cluster of red berries on the swatch of white cloth was unmistakable. *Strawberry Fields Forever*. The words burned him now like acid, like the sweat searing his eyes, dissolved and re-formed through a devil's flood of unshakable images: *his wife's little Honda nestled in front of the Isuzu, already pointed back toward the highway; the dry leaves slashing his face; the hard jutting ears and brown-fuzzed corn silks bumping grotesquely against his flanks as he stumbled on.*

Strawberry Fields. He'd christened her new underwear himself in a cockeyed parody, a few months earlier, Beatling the refrain as she'd slipped them off after the department party they always threw to end the academic year.

Corn. Rusted strands of barbed wire. A trail poked by deer hooves that wound down through thick clumps of aspen and cedar. Gray rocks. The glint of water. The shredded, buck-savaged bark of a rubbed fir.

The boy slouched at the foot of the pool, toeing pebbles over the sand, a gold lure dangling from the tip of his spinning rod. The angler's throat tightened with rage as he pushed through the last clump of alder—recognized the Twins cap and shock of red hair curling down over the child's protruding ears.

"Mr. Quinn! You just come down from the field up there?" the boy cried out happily. "You seen my dad?"

The angler stood staring at the reedy, jeans-clad legs across the water. Felt the cork handle of the cheap rod quiver in his hand.

"How did you get across the stream, Todd?"

The boy peered at him intently, startled by his curtness.

"My dad carried me," he finally answered. "Before he went back up to get the bag of stuff we forgot . . . the Cokes and the candy. But that was a long time ago."

For half a minute neither of them spoke again. There was only the quiet burble of the water and the roistering squawk of a bluejay somewhere back in the pines. The angler stared down at his shaking hands, their flesh pale and aging, blue veins webbing thinly beneath his skin. He shook open the pill box, let the tiny fly drop onto his fingers. Cradling the rod butt against his forearm, he labored numbly to tie on a tippet and stab it through the corroding hook's uptilted eye.

The confused boy looked past him, back up the trail, then leaned his own rod against a log and resumed idly tossing stones into the downstream riffle. Tiring of that, he again lifted the rod and shot a half-hearted cast across the lower end of the pool. The lure splashed down heavily a few yards from where the angler stood.

Another desultory cast followed, then another, each made with less enthusiasm than the one before. The lure wobbled back through the shallow water, shimmying and jerking to the raspy clicks of the sand-crusted reel.

"Why aren't you in school?"

The words sounded foreign to the angler's own ear, hard as boot soles, and the twelve-year-old again stared back at him hard. Water dripped from the silver spinner dangling below the tip of the rod.

"I don't have school today," he finally mumbled, the syllables climbing a scale of defensiveness that hung in the air as palpably as the luminous droplets trickling off the lure.

"It's Columbus Day," the boy added, slightly less defiantly. "Dad didn't know it either. . . . He couldn't believe it when he came home to get his stuff and saw me watchin' TV."

The angler glanced again at his hands, felt the clumsily knotted fly prick his thumb.

"You mean he hadn't planned to bring you along?"

"No. . . . He was actin' real weird . . . real diff'rent. I could tell he didn't want me to come with him at all. But I kept buggin' him. He hadn't took me for a long time. I just kept on buggin' him, you know. So did my mom."

The boy stopped and turned away—shot the lure aimlessly across the creek and muttered an audible obscenity as it hung up on the overhanging branch of a tamarack. The monofilament stretched as taut as a bowstring through the limpid air.

"I hate it here!" he cried, kicking at the sand. "It's boring! There's nothin' to catch. Alls you do is get your line tangled up and lose lures!" He punctuated the last word with a petulant jerk, snapping the line, which drifted limply downstream and trailed below him in the current. His dirt-smudged fingers tightened, then gradually went limp around the reel handle. A few seconds later he dropped the rod on the sand.

The angler stood silently watching him, his own fingers clenching and unclenching. When the scrawny frame slumped back and dropped on the log, he studied it a moment longer, then slowly stepped into the water. The lost lure hung head-high less than twenty feet upstream, shining in the warm, late afternoon sun.

But the water was cold. He took half a dozen shuffling steps and stopped, knee-deep in the pool.

Moments later it was his own line that kinked in the water behind him, coiling mutinously after years of neglect off the cheap, unused reel.

Taking what it would yield him through the rod guides, he false-cast several times, trying to work the kinks out, then targeted the undressed Adams at a shaded lie behind an upstream rock. The raggy fly parachuted down far short in loops of leader. The too-stiff rod twitched with alien insubordination in his hand.

Sitting motionless on the log, the boy studied him closely, his face dark and expressionless beneath the downturned brim of his cap. His thin legs looked as flimsy as shore reeds beneath the mud-crusted jeans.

The angler lifted the damp fly off the water, stripped off another coil or two of line—aimed another cast at the leaf-strewn rockface. This time the fly dropped lightly just below it and danced unmolested downstream.

The narrow, scrutinizing face watching him hadn't moved.

He made another half-dozen casts, inching forward, the spiral twists of shed line trailing in the current behind him. A chill like death had begun to creep up his thighs.

Rod pinched between his chest and forearm, he slowly turned and peered back into the tight freckled face, whose hard gaze hadn't wavered. For some time the two of them stared at each other, man and boy, neither of them speaking.

It was the man who finally spoke.

"Have you ever cast a fly?"

The youth looked sharply away before answering, his eyes drifting back up the trail.

"No. . . . Dad says I'm not old enough. . . . He told me I could maybe try it next year—if I grow another inch or two."

The fisherman looked suddenly away too, toward the head of the pool, where a dimpled ring slowly spread over the glassy surface of the water. Instinctively he felt his pulse quicken. *Even here,* the thought faintly registered. *Even now.*

The words that followed seemed to come just as instinctively, mechanical as the silent lift and pause of his casting arm.

"Mike had his own rod when he was eight, the one I'm holding. He caught a sixteen-inch brown on it a week after he turned ten."

The boy's eyes drifted away again, toward the distant field on the ridge, and even across the burbling stream he could hear the child's muffled snuffle. He hadn't meant to hurt him. Not consciously. A lifetime earlier, up in the corn, thoughts and words and intentions had melted together like a Dali clock.

"Listen," he heard his voice continue, distant as the slanting rays of dying sun filtering down through the trees on the ridge. "You're big enough. You're old enough. Come on out here and we'll give it a try."

The boy wiped his nose on his shoulder, hesitated. The angler took a step back down the stream toward him, beckoned him on with his hand.

"Move as quietly as you can through the water. A couple of fish have started rising. Move quietly but quickly. . . . Evening's coming on."

The groan was audible when the sneakered feet slid into the stream, but they crept on as the tremulous voice quavered "It's *cold*! It's so *cold* on my legs."

The angler's own legs felt anesthetized as he waited, studied the approaching boy's thin face—draped a hand over the sparrowy shoulders and rubbed them into warmth when the shaking limbs finally leaned into his hip. There the two of them stood for a moment, holding in the current, staring down at the water that lipped above the man's kneecaps and sluiced around the skittish child's groin.

"Okay," the fisherman murmured, settling the rod in the boy's quivering fingers. "You've been watching me do it. Keep that image in your brain, like a photograph, as I tell you the couple of things you'll need to know."

He felt the muscles tighten like wire across his gut as he said it, a bitter coppery taste rise in his throat.

"First, when you take the rod back, I want you to stop it above your head—even though that will seem unnatural. Stop it like a clock stuck at noontime. That's not where it's going to stop, but it should feel like it. You do it because every beginner takes the rod back too far."

The boy nodded, eyes wide with anticipation and cold.

"Second, when you do stop the rod, stop it *hard*. The other mistake every beginner makes is to wave the rod back and forth, limply, like a wand.

"Finally, and this is the hardest to explain—but the way you were watching me, I think you caught it—your hand has to slant slightly up to down, up to down, as it moves back and forth over the water. Like this." He pumped the air with his rodless hand, canting the forward thrust downward. "Not like this."

The boy's face clouded, then cleared.

"It should feel a little like you're tossing a dart at that rock up ahead of us. If it feels like you're aiming a spear at that tree, you're doing it wrong."

The fisherman's voice broke as he said it, and he said no more, the first, tentative flailings of his own son fusing with the demon-images etched in his brain.

Five minutes later the stiff loops of leader tumbled down a yard behind the still rising trout, whose quick wake traced a faint, arrowing arc to the near shore. But the rod remained in the boy's hands. And most of the twenty feet of line on the water drifted back toward his quivering fingers in a sinewy curl.

The angler squeezed the bony shoulder, felt the seeping cold, the spasm of loss yet swelling joy in the breathless question.

"It's gone, isn't it? It's not going to rise anymore."

He stared at the dark water ahead of him, then back at the boy.

For the first time he noticed that the current was lapping just below the child's belt, its buckle gleaming like a diamond in the day's last fracturing glints of sunlight. Most of the pool now lay in shadow, though just above them the white bark of a birch shimmered and a tamarack dropped a phalanx of golden needles into the stream.

The breeze rose then in a whisper through the pines and he turned back to the shivering youth at his side.

"That's enough," he said softly. "You're getting the hang of it. Climb out and warm up in that patch of sun by the rocks, before it disappears too."

Teeth chattering, the boy peered up into his face for half a second, then handed him the rod gratefully and splashed out of the stream. The angler remained where he stood, his own limbs numb, his eyes fixed on the spectral birch boughs as the rod lay inert in his hand.

When the last ray of light dissolved over a hanging leaf, he turned abruptly and resumed casting, slowly stripping more and more line off the reel. Somewhere in the woods above them a bird fluttered, a loosed pebble clattered against a tree. The boy yelped on the shore behind him. Footsteps thudded heavily down the trail from the ridgetop. The fisherman let the rod work on, kept on casting, inching forward under the ring of bluffs walling off the world beyond them—let the line hiss on over the dark water flowing like the oils of Lethe around his numb, enervated loins.

Labor Day

Thanks to the end-of-summer holiday, they have a three-day weekend. Time off from her work at the county courthouse before his classes start in the fall. Time to finally "get away together," as they'd long falsely promised each other they wanted to do. What's been missing is trust, from each of them, and both of them know it. Their commitment has been simply words, comforting insulation, which has kept them from acknowledging the failure of their marriage, maybe even to themselves.

It's hard to say how, or even when, the rupture started. Gazing out of the car at the sun-splashed countryside, he remembers what it was like three decades earlier, the last time they made this drive. They'd been blindly in love then—trusted each other completely. Trusted enough that he'd asked her to go fishing with him, and she had eagerly agreed.

It would not have been a signal mark of trust for many couples here, in Minnesota, where he'd lived all his life. A wife might even ask her husband to *take* her fishing—might in fact have fished more than he. But his wife had grown up in the East—spent a college summer in France and even been to South America the year before he met her, though never anywhere west of Philadelphia in the United States. That back then she had been so excited to go up to the Brule with him has left a hole in his heart.

The car rolls on. She says nothing as they cross the silver bridge over the Mississippi, stares down at the water where a barge plunges downstream past a brushy island rimmed with sand. A houseboat bobs in the barge's wake, moored to the beach by a pair of white anchor ropes. Kids splash in the shallows along the shore.

"Great day to be on the river," he says, glancing across the seat at her face.

"Mmmm," she murmurs noncommittally, her eyes still fixed on the barge.

Half an hour later, rolling meadows and small dairy farms pass outside the windows. They're far enough north a few maples have started to redden. Several miles back up the road, they passed a cranberry bog, crimson as fresh blood.

"It's interesting here," she says quietly. The words are so welcome he says nothing, simply nods and drives on.

Finally he speaks. "It's like it was before," he says. "The day we drove up here, thirty years ago. Do you remember? It was a little later in September, but close to this time of year."

He regrets the words as soon as he says them. Regrets them even more when a guarded "uh-huh" is her only response.

How *had* it gone so bad? What flashes in his mind is the nightmarish day he found her screwing his best friend fifteen years earlier—the still searing image of her strawberry panties, draped over the seat of Dooley's van where they'd parked on the rutted lane by the field of corn. But that was effect, not cause. His own liaisons with students had preceded it, and there had been several more in the angry, silently vengeful aftermath.

It was even less clear to him how the healing had begun. Somehow it had, over the past year or so, though neither of them had verbally acknowledged it. Perhaps as they approached sixty the flames simply burned themselves out, both the anger and the lust. Yet the wounds remained so raw it was as if the slightest acknowledged tension might reopen them. Best simply not to question—let the fragile mending continue, however it would.

Glancing at her impassive face again, he wonders if she's remembering that earlier trip, as he is. And if she is, whether the memory is anything like his own. He's thought of it so often, in the three decades since, the images seem less like memory than a photograph or painting. A kaleidoscope of scenes etched in the brain.

The new tent, blue and silver, pitched in perfect taut lines under the pines beside the shimmering river. The softness of the fallen needles beneath their feet as they pad to the stone fire ring by the shoreline. Her body, aroused and shivering, arching above him in the pale shafts of moonlight that flicker across her skin with the soughing of the wind through the trees.

The fishing came the next morning. Was it truly possible, as it has so long seemed to him, that nothing was ever the same between them again?

That he had been stupidly insensitive—self-absorbed to the point of obsession in his drive to fish—all of that he's long privately acknowledged. He had fished the Brule only once before, the autumn before he met her, and the lure of the river and the single bright steelhead he had taken from it were like nothing he had ever experienced before. The fish was not large, no more than five or six pounds. But the way it had taken the fly and shot out of the water had loosed a kind of demon in his gut. Back then, even in those first idyllic months of their marriage, he was no more capable of ignoring it than he'd been of turning away from that smoldering sex in their tent.

And so they had fished. Or rather, he had fished. Crept intently down the river working the fly while she walked the trail alongshore. But there was no trail—no trail, at least, that she would have recognized as such back in the benign terrain where she'd grown up in Massachusetts. There *had* been a worn path into the woods from their campsite. But he should have known it would soon peter out to nothing more than a faint animal track—would leave her to stoop and push her way through overhanging branches, thickets of alder, and ankle-deep muck.

He had short-hooked a steelhead that morning, but when he rejoined her an hour later he had lost far more than that bright, pulsing fish. And never since had things felt the way they had that preceding night in the tent, their depleted bodies sinking back into the warmth of the sleeping bags as their breath rose visibly in the chill autumn air.

The silence, the train of thought and memory, have held him so long it feels as if they've entered another country when awareness returns of the land outside the car. Birches and aspen. Cattails in the ditches. And where the soil is drier, the delicate lavender blossoms of fireweed. The golden needles of tamarack glow through the woods where narrow unpaved lanes vanish into the shadows, the unseen cabins signaled by a painted moose or a northern pike or bear cubs above the owners' name woodburned on a mailbox or a hung cedar plank: *The Weavers. The Johnsons. Ted and Marcia Auerbach.*

He drives on, down a stretch of untrafficked blacktop where the encroaching woods are broken only with the occasional human reminder: *Carl's Watch & Chainsaw Repair. The Backwoods Motel. Tucker's Scales & Claws—Taxidermy.*

It's been so long since either of them has spoken her voice startles him, though it is soft, her face still turned toward the window.

"Castaways from Lake Wobegon."

Still a little disoriented, he's unsure of her tone. Sarcastic? Amused but nostalgic? He remains uncertain when she speaks again.

"Do you want to stop for lunch?"

He glances at the dashboard clock. The fact that it's almost two in the afternoon jolts him further. More than three hours have passed since they crossed the Mississippi, peered down at the barge.

"Sure," he says, pulling off the blacktop into the parking lot of the timbered tavern at the edge of the woods. You saw them often in this remote country south of Lake Superior, roadside haunts in the middle of nowhere that beckoned locals and the occasional passerby—beacons through the frigid, eternal winter days and nights. The sign above this one, flanked by a pair of painted Packer helmets, reads *The Wiscy Beer House.*

He leads her inside and they sit down in a pine booth opposite the bar, where a jowly man slouches on a silver-legged stool. The pallid flesh beneath his undersized T-shirt bulges like a life preserver. A neon Miller High Life sign on the wall casts an orange glow over shelved bottles of liquor. Beside it, a black-lettered placard reads "Live Hard. Die Hard. Stay Hard."

"Classy place," his wife murmurs, glancing at him across the pocked linoleum tabletop. But there's a faint smile on her lips, and the words hold little or none of their accustomed sting. Or has he only imagined it—the after-effect of his long daydream in the car?

The bartender is a woman he guesses to be in her fifties, though it's difficult to tell. She could be a decade older or younger. Her hair is dyed black and her teeth nicotine-stained, a blue panda bear inked just above her left ankle. She smiles crookedly as she reaches their booth.

"What'll it be, sweetie?" she says to his wife.

He cringes—knows the word is grating on her like jagged glass. Dreads the reaction, visual and possibly even verbal, that's sure to come. But somehow it doesn't. His wife orders a light beer and a hamburger. So imperceptible was the slight tightening of her jawline he thinks he alone could have noticed it.

"And how about you, darlin'?" the woman turns to him, grinning.

Had she noticed it? Called him that simply to annoy his wife? Or is it just the way the local women talk to men up here?

Numb, he mumbles his order—a draft beer and a burger with onions—turns again to his wife as the woman walks back across the grimy floor to the bar. They watch silently as a pair of even beefier men in checkered shirts enter the room and drop on barstools beside the other. Laughter and a raspy cough fuse with their guttural voices and the sudden sizzle of the frying burgers in the stale air.

"Interesting place," he says, smiling ironically.

"I think it *is* interesting, actually," she says, her eyes fixed on the three men, one of whom rolls a pair of dice out of a worn leather cup onto the bar. "It feels authentic. Genuine. I don't know about that woman though," she adds, smiling archly. "I think she was giving you the eye."

He doesn't know how to respond, it's been so long since he's seen this side of her. Teasing, playfully seductive. Or is that how she meant it? Could he have misinterpreted that too?

"Fat chance," he says finally. "I think one of those dudes at the bar is more her style."

"They're fat all right."

"Livin' off the fat o' the land."

"Ruffed grouse and snowshoe rabbits. Maybe one of those fish you were so desperate to catch the last time. What was its name? Ironhead?"

He knows the last is teasing, but again he's slow to respond. Remains uncertain of her intentions. Before he can speak she goes on.

143

"Seriously, I wonder what these people *do* up here—how they survive. There doesn't seem to be any agriculture to speak of. No visible industry. And yet the roads are paved and the houses and trailers look reasonably well kept for the most part. Places like this one seem to have enough business to hang on. It's bewildering to me."

"I've always wondered that too," he responds quickly—honestly. "From the first time I ever came up here, the year before we met. It's hard to believe, but not much seems to have changed since then, at least not much that I can see. It's one of the things I like best about the place."

She is about to speak, say something more, when the waitress returns with the burgers and beer. "Enjoy," she says simply, still smiling, and turns to leave.

"Thanks, they look delicious," his wife says, stopping her. She pauses as the woman turns, the smile warming on her face. "We're both curious," his wife adds, a little awkwardly, clearing her throat. "How do people make a living up here, in this country. I mean, it's beautiful—I can see why you'd want to live here, but . . ."

She stops, clearly at a loss how to go on.

He remains dazed. It's not that he's never seen this side of her—this spontaneous risk taking—even in the long, alienated blight of their past. Four years earlier, on vacation in Ireland, he'd sat astonished as she rose in a Dingle pub and sang a Gaelic dirge he didn't know she knew at a wake for a friend of the half-drunk locals, who sat listening dubiously, then slowly quieted, grew rapt. Some would have called her act foolhardy, or condescending. He'd recognized it as the mourners had—a gesture of genuine sympathy and courage. As far beyond his compass, as defiant of convention, as screwing your husband's best friend.

Not for the first time in the thirty years he'd known her, he felt how hopelessly he'd fallen under her spell.

"It's a good question," the waitress answers. "Ask anybody who comes in here and they'll all tell you we're crazy. But none of us seem able to leave."

"I understand that," his wife answers. "I do."

The two men who entered the bar last drop some money beside their empty bottles and walk out, their heavy boots thudding across the floorboards. He and his wife follow soon after. He leaves a generous tip between their emptied plates.

They drive on up the county highway with its unnumbered road signs marked simply "H." The sun has dropped noticeably in the western sky.

"The Apostles should be lovely this time of the year," he says to her. "I'm glad we finally decided to go."

"Mmmm," she murmurs, staring out at the pines and tamaracks. A lone maple rises close to the road ahead of them, its fallen leaves carpeting the blacktop a glowing red. He stares across the car at her, on the verge of speaking—notices again the strands of gray that have recently appeared in her thick hair. He says nothing, drives on.

An hour before sunset they reach Highway 2 and turn right, a dozen miles from the Lake Superior shore. Brule is less than fifteen minutes ahead—the tiny village and the hypnotic river—the place he'd first crossed it that summer before he met her, when he'd risen before dawn and fished two-thirds of the way down to the big lake the next day. The kid that filled his car with gas that night hadn't believed he could have covered so much distance—fished past "the Ledges" and "the Boxcars" and beyond. Clearly, nothing in the youth's world of experience had let him conceive of a man so taken with the stream and its elusive rainbows that miles and hours could dissolve like oxygen in his fevered blood.

It astounds him too now, the fact that he'd done it—fished seven or eight miles of rocky river hoping for a single strike. The kid had stared at him as if he were crazy, seemed finally to believe him, but obviously thought he was nuts.

And maybe he was nuts, all those years ago, when both his fishing and his appetite for sex were insatiable. If he hadn't had three classes to teach at the university—needed to drive the seven hours back home—he'd have risen the next morning and fished the same stretch of water again. Just as, back then, he would have screwed even more women if the chance arose.

But all that was behind him now. At least the capacity, if not quite all of the desire. Maybe that was the single gift age brought. The compensations. For that's exactly how he's come to think of it, staring out at the scenic expanse of trees and sky he would barely have noticed even five years before. He glances again at his wife. Her gaze is fixed out the opposite window. Briefly his heart lifts with the feeling that here, at least, after so many years of alienation, they seem to have arrived at a point where their pulses can beat as one.

Brule 5.

The roadside sign flashes past and diminishes in the rearview mirror—leaves a visceral surge that flows from his loins into his chest. For the first time in weeks—the night he had made the initial, tentative suggestion of the trip—he suddenly feels himself wanting, *aching*, to fish. The word that leaps instantly into his consciousness is *delusion*—the conviction that what he'd felt all those years earlier was behind him, that there was some "compensation" for leaving his youth behind. The desire to fish again—to fish the *Brule* again—sweeps through him. It is simultaneously one of the most stirring and depressing feelings of his life.

He drives on, through the evening shadows. Five minutes later the village sign appears, then the familiar stone bridge, and he glimpses the gleaming water beneath it as they pass. A hundred yards farther on, where the township road stretches left across the single set of railroad tracks toward Lake Superior, his wife turns to him and says sharply, *"Stop."*

He pulls off on the shoulder, bewildered. There is nothing in the village but the gas station and a few scattered buildings—the vast northern woods stretching west and north around the lake into Canada and beyond.

"This is the little town you brought me to, isn't it?" she says to him. The words don't sound accusatory, but he's not certain. The last few minutes have cost him whatever of his bearings remained intact.

"Yes," he answers. "This is Brule."

"Do you remember that campsite," she continues, "the one by the river, where we pitched your tent?"

"Yes," he says. "I remember it. It's three or four miles down that road."

He nods to the left as he says it, across the railroad tracks, toward the huge, frigid lake.

"Let's go there," she says quietly, her face turning away from him. "I want to see what it's like now."

He says nothing, silently obeys her. Turns the car over the track and up the narrow road beyond the town.

It surprises, almost stuns him, how easily he finds it. The same trees. More fallen needles. Burbles of flowing water beside the tent site where he'd had the best lovemaking of his life. He pulls up next to the fire ring and switches off the ignition. For some time the two of them remain in the car, staring out at the river. An evening breeze soughs above them through the pines.

"It is lovely here," she says. "I'd almost forgotten."

"I fell in love with the Brule the moment I first saw it," he answers. "You probably know the lines from Wordsworth, *It is a beauteous evening, calm and free. The holy time is quiet as a Nun, breathless with adoration.* That's how it felt."

He stops, but she says nothing.

"There used to be a little motel back in the town, and this is the hour I first pulled up to it. I walked back up the highway, to the bridge, and stared down into the water. I stood there until it got dark, before I checked in."

Neither of them says anything more for several minutes. A crow sails down from a pine and begins pecking at the ground in front of them. A chipmunk scampers across a rotting log near the stream.

"I want you to teach me how to fly fish," she says abruptly.

He stares at her, disbelieving, the soft words not registering in his brain.

"What?" he says, numb.

"I want you to show me how to fly fish," she repeats, louder, turning toward him. "Right here. Right now."

The confirmation is so stunning he doesn't know how to react. Their plan was to drive on for at least another hour. Find a lakeside motel and then catch the ferry out to the Apostle Islands early the next day. Yes, he has a fly rod in the trunk—there is always a fly rod in his trunk—but he hasn't planned on anything like this, even the remote possibility of its ever happening. For that much, at least, his conscience is clear. For a fleeting moment Freud's famous quote flashes across his fuddled mind: *What do women want?*

But he says nothing more—opens the door and walks back to the rear of the car for his vest and the little four-weight rod in its silver tube. When he turns back she is standing on the bed of pine needles, gazing out at the river. He stops a few yards behind her, his eyes fixed on her back, her body still as lithe and graceful as a dancer's. Slowly he strings the rod and then moves on to her side.

For a long moment they remain there, gazing at the water. A few strands of moss weave like mirages in the current beneath the glassy surface.

"Okay," he finally murmurs, as she turns to face him. "Before you begin, there are a couple of things you'll need to know . . ."

The Rod

Just below the sloping lawn, down on the lake, a small boat is trolling for walleyes. The pair of shirt-sleeved fishermen are seated. When the boat turns, retraces its course, their lines glint briefly in the sun.

The woman sitting alone on her deck continues to gaze at them, at the shimmering water. Several years earlier, pressed by her husband, she had gone out on a fishing boat for the only time in her life. They too were trolling. She hadn't gotten seasick, as she feared she would, and he had accomplished what he'd hoped to—caught and released a large, leaping sailfish. But the experience had left him nearly as unimpressed as she had been—so indifferent he'd forfeited the prepaid fee and canceled the trip he'd booked for the following morning. "That's it for me," he said to her, stepping back onto the dock. "I'd forgotten how trapped I feel. Bored. Always have, even in my childhood. I have to be walking, *moving*—fishing a stream."

Was it in fact the last time in his life he had been in a boat, that February in 2002 when they'd fled the frigid Minnesota winter for a week in Mexico? What she remembers most of Zihuatanejo is not the things she liked the most—the lovely, palm-fringed beach below their rented condo; the gentleness of the local people, even the young fathers with their children; the walk along the curving *bahia* into town. What comes back to her viscerally now is the thunderstorm the day after he'd caught the sailfish, when the rain began to fall before dawn and then kept on falling until it sluiced above their ankles down the sloping streets as they sloshed along, in search of an open restaurant, wearing the black plastic bags he'd pierced with arm and neck holes. His childish

149

glee, the gravelly sound of his laughter. The look on his face when they splashed back into the condo, soaked to the skin, and he stared out at the churning surf lapping the dark sand of La Madera fifty yards below. The rod was out of his suitcase before she had stripped and changed into dry clothes. The rod that was always with him, wherever they traveled, in its little silver tube beside the green cloth reel sack and the plastic box of assorted flies.

Literally *always*. Tucked away in his car trunk or the suitcase, and even once, when they'd hiked down into the Grand Canyon, strapped to his back. At *pensiones* in the Dolomites. Plank-floored *zimmers* in Germany. Too many French *logis* and British B&B's to count. How often had he wakened before dawn, in their thirty-two years of marriage—climbed out of their bed and crept off to fish some obscure mountain stream or clear-flowing Scottish burn they'd happened on in their rental car? How often braked to a stop on a bridge or pulled abruptly off on the shoulder so he could peer down at the current, searching for the ephemeral, flitting shadow of a trout. If there had been a trout stream on campus, she'd once said to him with an edge of bitterness, he'd have kept the rod in his office. She had thought she was joking, however icily. But the frozen expression on his face said at once that he'd considered it, possibly even had in fact stored one there.

And always too without a license. It was yet another of the countless contradictory things about him, quirks no one who knew him could fathom at all. A man scrupulous to a fault in his general treatment of people, the preparation and teaching of his classes, even the purchasing of licenses for any *planned* fishing trip longer than an hour or two. But for those *serendipitous* moments when he chanced on a stream that might hold trout, he'd been as untroubled, as guiltless as she felt sure he remained to the end of his life for the coeds he had screwed through all but the last few years of their marriage. Their *only* years of marriage, to be honest, in any true sense of the word.

The bitter acknowledgment stings her eyes, burns in them like acid. That he'd been conscientious and self-disciplined enough to keep his hands off them while they were still in one of his classes had only fueled her resentment, her maddening inability to comprehend.

The trolling boat makes another slow turn on the lake in front of her. A pair of hummingbirds hover off the deck's sugar-water feeder as the tears wet her face. So absorbed is she in the memories, the grief and anger, she is only distantly aware of them. *A lifetime of impulse. Impulse and excess. And also of kindness, just as reflexive. Endless phone and e-mail exchanges with his students, male and female. Too many pesos and zlotys and Euros handed to beggars and buskers on foreign streets and beaches to count.*

"God damn you, Patrick," the words barely audible. *"God damn you, Patrick Quinn."*

License. Not for the first time since his sudden death from a heart attack two weeks earlier, the irony stings her—the lines from one of his favorite poems, Donne's "To His Mistress, Going to Bed." He'd teasingly whispered them in her ear so often in the months before and after their marriage she had memorized them without trying to. *License my roving hands, and let them go / Before, behind, above, between, below. / O my America! My new-found land.*

Anger surges through her again at the recollection—his countless acts of license, of *licentiousness*, fusing with her grief. Grief both for her sudden loss and the fact he couldn't seem to help himself, so much did that boyish impetuosity lie at the center of his being—to the last day of his life, every experience he truly valued, somehow fresh and new. A trout stream or an attractive woman, there was little difference. Either one was a *new-found land.*

Again she thinks of Mexico. Zihuatanejo. Of his bare feet squishing back out the iron-grated door of their condo five minutes after they'd returned to it—the manic grin on his rain-streaked face as he carried the little rod and box of flies down the stone steps to the bay. *His tall, gangly frame awash to the armpits as the waves crash around him. The rhythmic swing of the rod over the water through the hard, unseasonable rain that continues to pour down.*

Five minutes later he had actually hooked something. The fact had never surprised her before for she knew he was a skilled fisherman— believed him when he returned to their hotel in Switzerland or France or the Czech Republic and said he'd caught and released two or fifteen or four. But the incongruous sight of him below the balcony where she'd remained against her will, watching—the heavy surf sloshing him toward the beach and back out again while the frail rod continued to swing through the pounding rain. . . .

It had seemed impossible to her then. Hooking a fish.

She closes her eyes at the memory. *The rod bent almost double, his right arm high over the rolling water . . . then higher still as a wave breaks, staggering him, before it rolls on and crashes onto the shore.*

When his body emerged out of the foam again he was still clutching it, but whatever fish he had briefly hooked was clearly gone. The lifted rod stood straight now above his head. And still he fished. His face, that big broad ruddy face that somehow remained young even as it wrinkled, still beaming when he finally returned, chilled and dripping, to the condominium.

"God, that was fun," he said, a grin spreading across it as he stripped off the soggy clothes and stood goose-fleshed and naked in front of her. "I don't know what the hell I had on, maybe a bonito or a sierra, possibly even a roosterfish. Whatever it was, he took off like a bat out of hell and broke me off about ten seconds after he felt the fly prick his lip."

Out on the lake, one of the fishermen has finally hooked a walleye. He stands in the back of the boat, reeling it in. A sob breaks suddenly from her chest as she watches him, then another, until she is crying uncontrollably. Crying as she'd never cried at the funeral or the moment four days earlier when they'd told her—his ashen-faced dean appearing at her desk in the courthouse to whisper solemnly that her husband had collapsed on the commons, died before the ambulance arrived.

The sobs continue to rack her body, ebb slowly down to nothingness. Rising unsteadily, she walks back through the house into the kitchen, opens the refrigerator, and bends to peer inside. A single beer remains from the last six-pack he ever bought. His favorite, a Sam Adams. Setting it on the counter, she walks on to the rear of the house and opens the door to his den.

It's the first time in months she has entered it—stood staring at the motley array of objects on the shelves and the cluttered desk. Stacks of books, both angling and academic. His tying vise. Scattered boxes of hooks and beads, threads and tinsel, patches of feathers and fur.

The rod case lies on a shelf above them, next to the green reel sack, where Mike or Danny had put them after cleaning out the trunk of his car. A few inches away, the Guinness pint glass rests near the wall.

Stepping past the clutter, she reaches up and takes all three of them down, closing the door behind her as she leaves the room. On the way back through the kitchen she picks up the beer and opens it, walks on — pauses only when her eye catches the flicker of her passing body in the hallway mirror. Stopping, she turns and stares at it. A woman of fifty-five, long past her prime, her face tear streaked and puffy. Her limbs tanned, still mostly unwrinkled. Her thick undyed hair streaked with gray.

She walks on and sits again in the deck chair, pours the beer into the glass. *One last one for you, Patrick*, she murmurs, closing her eyes and taking a long, grieving swallow. And still comes the licking flame of anger, there with the grief. The rod case lies on the deck beside her. She takes another deep swallow of the chilled beer. Then burns suddenly in her mind the distant afternoon when there was only anger. *Rage*. A rage so intense she'd committed the one truly treacherous act of her life.

Even then, in the full grip of her fury, she knew it never would have happened if she hadn't found the perfumed note in his shirt pocket. There had been students before, and he had admitted it. She had even cheated on him, once, soon after she'd learned of the first one, a brief liaison with a lawyer from the office down the hall.

But he was a relative stranger, to both of them. Dooley was her husband's best friend. And Annie was one of her own.

Staring out at the lake, she cringes at the memory. Closes her eyes again and takes another long swallow of the beer. *Doing it in the back of a van, cramped and sweating. Hidden away like felons down the muddy lane in a field of corn.*

It wouldn't have happened if she had known. Known where Dooley was leading her when he'd rolled too fast into the restaurant parking lot where she'd nervously agreed to meet him for a cup of coffee, quickly motioned her to follow him, and sped back down the highway in the direction from which he'd come.

It seems incredible to her now, the fact that she had gone along with it. Followed him down the rutted field lane and let him take her, almost literally, in the mud. The tears are flowing down her face again but this time the anger is directed not at her dead husband but herself. *Thank God he never learned of it.* The silent words flash like a prayer behind her swimming eyes. *Thank God for that.*

Yet with the anger and the guilt comes another emotion, more deeply buried, the cold awareness that had she not done something that vengeful she might never have been able to forgive him—finally get past the bitterness that had helped poison their marriage for years. She'd had no more affairs, even as she was sure he continued to have them. Had gone without satisfying sex, almost without sex of any kind, for so long it had stunned her the previous autumn when they'd taken the weekend trip up to the Apostle Islands and their lovemaking on successive nights in a woodsy motel room had swept her body back to the passions of her youth.

She stares down again at the tube on the deck beside her, remembers the last time she saw the rod it held. *The campsite on the Brule. The casting lesson she impulsively asked him to give her. The clumsiness, then the strange, growing thrill when the line begins to flow as if streaming organically out of her hand.*

Would any of it have happened, those last warm and intimate months, if it weren't for that quiet, restorative hour by the stream?

Setting the glass down by the chair, she lifts the hard little case off the deck and cradles it in her hands. The phallic symbolism is so obvious she bursts out laughing. "God damn you, Patrick," she repeats, still laughing—tears of laughter that fuse with the anger and the grief. Letting the tube drop into her lap she picks up the glass again and swallows the last few gulps of the beer. The empty glass remains in her hand, gleaming in the late afternoon sun.

There comes now another memory, just as vivid, as alive as the image of his big body leaning into the waves and driving rain. A different place, different time. They are on the coast of Ireland, a tiny village named Doolin. A few hundred yards from the inn where they are staying sits a small pub, perched along a cobblestone road above a small, clear stream that flows a short distance on into the sea. *Too many drafts of Smithwick's and Guinness. The wail of Irish folk music. Her husband rising suddenly, impulsively, in the middle of a fiddle solo—mumbling his familiar "back in a sec, my lovely" as he lopes out of the room and on up the road toward their inn.*

And he was in fact back quickly, holding what she knew he'd be holding, the little silver tube in his big-knuckled hand. The memory remains so sharp she can almost hear the fiddle playing on in her ear, see the grin of anticipation on his face.

Quaffing another half-dozen quick gulps of the lager, he steps back out of the pub and hops down over the low stone wall across the road from it— disappears from her view through the lead-mullioned window. Seething, she pays their tab and follows—stands on the road staring down at him as he casts into the pool below the stone bridge and on the first cast hooks a trout about ten inches long. Beaming up at her as he lands it, he holds its twitching side toward her in the late afternoon sunlight, its bright orange spots clearly visible even from where she stands twenty yards away. Releasing it, he continues to fish, soon catches another slightly larger trout and slips this one too back into the stream.

It was far from the first time she had lingered against her will, watching him cast, held by the outflowing line much as the throbbing strings of a cello or the arc of a flamenco dancer's lifted arms could hold her. Finally turning away, she had taken several angry steps up the road when she heard him yelp with childish pleasure—knew he must have hooked yet another, still bigger fish. But that wasn't it. As she walked on she heard him bounding up behind her, the old pair of tennis shoes he always also carried in his suitcase slapping wetly on the hard gray stones. *"So you'd be leavin' me, would you, lassie?"* he sang out in his parodic Irish accent. *"Look at this, ay? Kenna what your good man's been findin' now. Found it lyin' in the stream, he did."* In his hoisted fist, dripping on her feet, a slime-caked Guinness glass. Unbroken, not even cracked under the grime.

It's the gleaming glass she holds now in her own quavering hand. Dropped or tossed by some drunk or tipsy celebrant into the pool a week or month or years earlier, somehow unshattered, still intact. Walking on over the cobblestones, she had tried to convince him to return it. But she knew the chances he'd agree were about as likely as him turning away from those willing student dalliances years before. *Windfalls.* They lay forever outside his moral compass, alien as the possibility of passing any serendipitous brook or river, the absence of a legal license be damned. Back in the inn, he'd spent nearly an hour at the tiny sink, scraping and scrubbing until his knuckles were red and the glass shone like crystal in his hand.

She glances down again at the glass. Wipes a fleck of foam from its rim and sets it on the deck. Before the tears can start once more she picks up the rod case and quickly opens it—removes the felt wrapping with its red silk ribbons tied neatly in a bow. The almost weightless sections slide easily from their sleeves when she unrolls it. Dropping the wrap and case on the chair, she steps off the deck onto the cool grass— walks barefoot down the slope to the lakeshore. The trolling boat has gone but it wouldn't have mattered. She cares nothing now about how she appears.

The five short shafts of graphite rest in her hand. Carefully she fits them together—aligns the wire loops to receive the line. When the rod is assembled she takes the reel from her pocket and attaches it, then feeds the line up through the rings of wire. "Stringing," he had called it, the image of something fine grained and deeply treasured, a cello or a violin, flitting through her mind. For a long moment she stands there on the sand, trying to remember—remember all that had followed, that quiet evening beside the Brule River. Then the line is feeding through her fingers off the chattering reel as the rod lifts and his words rise to consciousness: *"Count two beats to let the line load. Two. Stop the rod at twelve o'clock and stop it hard. It will go farther than that but it should feel like it's straight above you because the other mistake every beginner makes is taking it back too far."*

And she does begin to feel it, the shaft of the rod tightening the line against its flexing resistance, feels the coils begin to flow over the lake in searching rhythms that dance like wraiths in her tear-stained eyes.

Season's End

The township road bends sharply away from the highway, curls past the rusting cages of an abandoned mink farm, then drops into the valley alongside the stream. On the final day of September, the last of the season, the angler peers anxiously through the rain-streaked windshield to get a first look at the water. For a week the sodden skies have hung over the farmland, unloading periodic showers without moving on, and he tenses against the sight of a cocoa-colored torrent flecked with foam. But the water is dark, a gunmetal reflection of the skies. Though a harrowing west wind rakes the stream's surface, his hands relax on the steering wheel. He'll be able to fish.

It is not the ending he would have chosen. In the Closing Day of the Mind the stream flows out of a languid summer into slanted rays of October sunlight. The fly line unfurls over water that gleams like cut crystal, its surface broken only by fluttering reds and golds dropped from a streamside maple tree. In the Closing Day of the Mind bees drone in blooms of wild aster, hawks trace wide looping arcs on the thermals, and the trout drift lazily from awnings of shore grass to pluck a last grasshopper or ant as it floats by.

The car rolls on through the drizzle, over a leaf-matted roadbed carpeted by cottonwoods and aspen, past farmhouses where wisps of smoke billowing from the chimneys are the only signs of life. It slows to a stop by a pasture gate. A hundred yards beyond sits another farmstead, usually bustling with barking dogs and the clank of machinery, now hunkered down quietly in the wind.

The stream lies at the bottom of a cattle path, muddied to midankle by the hooves of the pasture's Holsteins. Feeling nearly as bovine in his heavy sweater and mud-caked hip boots, the angler crosses where the cows have crossed to the opposite bank. Though the riffle is barely knee-deep, he is wheezing slightly as he struggles for footing. Is it the boots—so unwieldy after the freedom of a summer spent wading wet in a pair of sneakers—or the faint whisper of Time? In his breast pocket are the reading glasses to which, after months of vain procrastination, he recently surrendered. Threading line now through the rod guides, he remembers their first intimation: a June dusk, a tiny midge held at arm's length toward the fading light, and a tippet that stubbornly refused to find its way through the eye.

He makes three or four false casts, feeding out line. Though the clouds droop so low it seems he might snag one on a backcast, conditions have moderately improved. The drizzle has stopped, and the wind rakes up spray only in occasional gusts. On each cast he has to *throw* the fly into its buffets, driving the rod hard with his forearm. But if he does it right—waits an extra half-second for the weighted nymph to clear behind him—the line straightens and the fly burrows past his hat brim in a gratifying hiss.

For two hours he fishes without a strike, often distracted. At the first wooded bend a blue heron lifts off the water, *skrank-skranking* at his eviction from a choice elbow pool. The leaves of an adjacent cornfield rustle continuously, then explode as a huge flock of starlings rise and peel away in the wind, drifting across the valley for a half-minute like tattered shreds of black cloth. A few of his casts bore through to their target. Far more parachute down short amid limp coils of leader, or shoot long as he overcompensates and snags weeds on the opposite shore. More than one self-entangles on the rod guides as he loses tempo in a sudden gust.

Finally he lays the rod down. From inside his vest he extracts a peanut butter sandwich wrapped in wax paper, squeezed flat as pita bread but still dry. The stream's three best pools are behind him, wind-whipped and whiplashed by errant casts and fouled line. The hip boots, one with a pinhole leak that has soaked his leg to the knee, drag like cement shoes. Ahead lies a long expanse of dead water he's fished with minimal success for years.

It is less a pool than a trough, chest-deep in places but sluggish as a Louisiana bayou. In midsummer a dry fly alights and expires, inert on the overheated water, while a nymph splashes down and sinks at once to the bottom moss.

But this isn't midsummer, he tells himself, finishing the sandwich and stowing the wrapping in his pocket. The moss is gone and the water is cold.

Analytical or self-deluded, he ties on a black Woolly Worm and again resumes casting from the shore. The wind, now quartering downstream, drags the weighted fly as it bellies the floating line across the choppy surface. The angler's eyes squint to focus on the white strike indicator where the line joins the leader. On the third cast when it pauses in middrift, he sets the hook hopefully and hauls to shore a waterlogged willow. Still, he has a heightened sense of possibility. Except when the harshest gusts send the line skittering wildly across the water, it hugs the surface in a satisfying full-bellied arc, the nymph trailing near the bottom at a tempting creep.

He fishes slowly on, his eyes so intent on the tiny white indicator they begin to tear. Again comes the pause, almost imperceptible in the chop, and he strikes once more. This time the line throbs, the rod arches, and a hooked fish flashes above the mud on the bottom. Two minutes later the brown trout lies on the grass at his feet, a fat female of about seventeen inches, her golden pectoral fins edged with ivory and her sides dappled in orange and red.

Momentarily subdued, the fish lies quietly, a slash of color on grass blades still glazed by the rain. It is too perfect, this image that somehow saddens as it thrills. Deep in the angler's stream of consciousness the poem flashes and rolls: *so much depends on a red wheelbarrow glazed with rain water* . . .

Season's end. A half-year from a new beginning.

He looks hard at the fish. Hauled from the freezer in the darkness of a northern winter, the ice-sheath would melt and the dead, hoarfrosted flesh would thaw—transmute once again into gold. An alchemy.

For a long moment he wants the fish with an intensity beyond comprehension.

Then, as suddenly as it came, the moment passes. When he removes the hook the trout flops heavily toward the water, her belly sagging with the flamboyant egg sacs that would burst like embers from the slit made by his knife. If the few hours that remain hold fish still to be caught in the winds of autumn, he'll keep one or two ten-inchers for that midwinter meal—serve them with a good white wine.

But not this one.